PENGUIN BOOKS

SYLVIA AND CHRISTABEL PANKHURST

Barbara Castle was educated at Bradford Girls' Grammar School and St Hugh's College, Oxford, and was a Member of Parliament from 1945 to 1979. She was a member of the National Executive Committee of the Labour Party from 1950 to 1984, becoming Chairman of the Labour Party (1958–9). She held four Cabinet posts in Harold Wilson's Governments of 1964–70 and 1974–6. She has been a member of the European Parliament since 1979 and is currently Member for Greater Manchester West. *The Castle Diaries* have been published in two volumes, the first in 1980 and the second in 1984.

LIVES OF MODERN WOMEN

General Editor: Emma Tennant

Lives of Modern Women is a series of short biographical portraits by distinguished writers of women whose ideas, struggles and creative talents have made a significant contribution to the way we think and live now.

It is hoped that both the fascination of comparing the aims, ideals, set-backs and achievements of those who confronted and contributed to a world in transition and the high quality of writing and insight will encourage the reader to delve further into the lives and work of some of this century's most extraordinary and necessary women.

Barbara Castle

Sylvia and Christabel Pankhurst

Penguin Books

Penguin Books Ltd, Harmondsworth, Middlesex, England
Viking Penguin Inc., 40 West 23rd Street, New York 10010, USA
Penguin Books Australia Ltd, Ringwood, Victoria, Australia
Penguin Books Canada Ltd, 2801 John Street, Markham, Ontario, Canada L3R 1B4
Penguin Books (NZ) Ltd, 182–190 Wairau Road, Auckland 10, New Zealand

Published in Penguin Books 1987
Copyright © Barbara Castle, 1987

Grateful acknowledgement is made to the following:

For extracts from *The Suffragette Movement: An Intimate Account of Persons and Ideals*
(1931) by Sylvia Pankhurst to Longman Group Ltd;
For extracts from *Unshackled: The Story of How We Won the Vote* (1959) by
Christabel Pankhurst to Hutchinson, an imprint of Century Hutchinson;
For extracts from unpublished material by Sylvia Pankhurst in the Institute of
Social History, Amsterdam, to Richard Pankhurst.

Filmset in 10 on 13 pt Monophoto Photina

Made and printed in Great Britain by
Richard Clay Ltd, Bungay, Suffolk

CONTENTS

SYLVIA AND CHRISTABEL PANKHURST

The four line drawings that appear in the text are reproduced courtesy of Mary Evans/Fawcett Library.

ACKNOWLEDGEMENTS

My warmest thanks must go to the Fawcett Library in the City of London Polytechnic for their generosity and patience in giving me access to so many books, many of which are out of print. I am grateful for the help they gave my research assistant, Anita Pollack, in turning up in their files the cuttings I needed of Christabel's and other people's articles. I hope it will not be long before the Fawcett Library is able to rehouse its archives as spaciously as they deserve to be.

I am also grateful to Mien Schreuder of the Institute of Social History, Amsterdam, for helping me find my way through Sylvia Pankhurst's personal papers.

My thanks to Anita Pollack for her efficient research and to Alen Mathewson, who competently took over from Anita while she had her baby. I am also indebted to my incomparable secretary, Joan Woodman, who typed away at all hours and helped me to piece this book together.

1865   Manchester National Society for Women's Suffrage
        formed with Dr Richard Pankhurst's help.
1879   Emmeline Goulden marries Richard Pankhurst.
1880   Christabel Pankhurst born in Manchester.
1882   Sylvia Pankhurst born in Manchester.
1885   Pankhursts move to London.
1892   Keir Hardie elected to Parliament. Helps to found
        the Independent Labour Party (ILP) the following
        year.
1893   Pankhursts return to Manchester. Emmeline and Richard
        join ILP.
1897   National Union of Women's Suffrage Societies (NUWSS)
        formed.
1898   Richard Pankhurst dies.
1900   Sylvia wins scholarship to Manchester School of Art.
1902   Sylvia wins travelling studentship and goes to Venice to
        study art.
1903   Sylvia decorates hall in Salford erected by ILP to her
        father's memory; women barred. Indignant Emmeline
        Pankhurst forms Women's Social and Political Union
        (WSPU).
1904   Christabel meets Eva Gore-Booth and Esther Roper of the
        North of England Women's Suffrage Society and becomes

active in women's suffrage campaign. Decides to study law at Manchester University.

1905　Bamford Slack's Bill for women's suffrage talked out in Commons. Militant tactics begin. Christabel interrupts Liberal meeting at Free Trade Hall, Manchester; sent to prison for 'assaulting' the police.

1906　Liberals come to power under Campbell-Bannerman. WSPU decides to move its activities to London. The Pethick-Lawrences give it accommodation at Clements Inn. Emmeline Pethick-Lawrence becomes its treasurer. Women invade lobby of House of Commons. The militants dubbed 'Suffragettes' by the *Daily Mail*.

1907　The first 'Women's Parliament' held at Caxton Hall. Deputation to House of Commons brutally broken up. Sylvia and Christabel go to prison again. The Pethick-Lawrences found *Votes for Women* newspaper. Christabel and Emmeline Pankhurst resign from ILP.

1908　Asquith becomes Liberal Prime Minister; declares his opposition to votes for women. Massive women's demonstration in Hyde Park. Suffragettes harry Liberal ministers. At a Trafalgar Square rally with her mother and Flora Drummond, Christabel urges women to 'rush the House of Commons'. The three women are tried for conspiracy and sent to prison.

1909　Agitation stepped up. Policy of window breaking launched. Emmeline Pankhurst incites Suffragette prisoners to go on hunger strike to secure release. Forcible feeding of hunger strikers introduced.

1910　Government calls general election on Lords' issue. Liberals returned with reduced majority. 'Conciliation Bill' to give women a limited franchise introduced. Government refuses to give it facilities. Women's deputation to House of Commons violently manhandled on 'Black Friday'. Asquith goes to country again on Lords' issue. Sylvia tours America.

1911　Liberals returned to power. Militants declare truce for Coronation. Asquith announces that a male Franchise Reform Bill will be introduced the following year and that a women's suffrage amendment to it could be moved. WSPU denounces it as a trick and ends truce.

1912　Militancy takes new and more violent form. Pethick-Lawrences, Emmeline Pankhurst and Christabel charged with conspiracy to incite persons to commit damage to property. Christabel flees to Paris. Breaks with Pethick-Lawrences over new militant policy. She and her mother launch the *Suffragette*. Sylvia intensifies women's suffrage campaign in East End. Asquith introduces men-only Franchise Reform Bill.

1913　Women's amendment to Franchise Reform Bill ruled out of order by the Speaker. Destructive militancy stepped up. In prison Sylvia goes on hunger and thirst strike and is forcibly fed. Growing public concern at forcible feeding. Government's response is the 'Cat-and-Mouse Act' under which hunger strikers released for short periods to regain their health and then rearrested. Emily Wilding Davison killed as she tries to stop the King's horse at the Derby. Christabel launches moral crusade in the *Suffragette*.

1914　Christabel breaks with Sylvia. Sylvia's East London Federation of the Suffragettes severed from the WSPU. She continues her East End activities and launches the *Workers' Dreadnought*. She threatens to continue her hunger and thirst strike to the point of death unless Asquith receives a deputation of East End women. Asquith relents and gives deputation the impression that his attitude is softening. First World War breaks out. Christabel returns to London. She and Emmeline Pankhurst suspend militancy and throw themselves behind war effort. Sylvia opposes the war and concentrates on her work in the East End.

1915 Keir Hardie dies.

1916 Speaker's Conference set up to discuss electoral reform.

1917 Speaker's Conference Report proposes votes for all men
over twenty-one and the enfranchisement of women on
more limited basis.

1918 Representation of the People Bill becomes law, giving the
vote at thirty to women householders or the wives of
householders, occupiers of land or premises of a
minimum value and university graduates. Act passed to
enable women to stand for Parliament. Armistice signed.
In general election Christabel fights Smethwick as Lloyd
George 'coupon' candidate. Loses by 775 votes. The
Countess Markievicz elected for Dublin constituency, but,
as a Sinn Fein leader, refuses to take her seat.

1919 Lady Astor elected to House of Commons in a by-
election. Sylvia teams up with Silvio Corio, an Italian
socialist. Declares herself a Bolshevik. Emmeline
Pankhurst lectures in America and Canada.

1920 Sylvia rechristens her former East London Federation the
'Communist Party'. Criticized by Lenin. Sentenced to six
months' imprisonment for sedition.

1921 Sylvia expelled from British Communist Party for attacks
on Lenin. Emmeline Pankhurst becomes lecturer for
National Council for Combating Venereal Diseases in
Canada. Joined by Christabel, who has become Second
Adventist. Christabel lectures on the Second Coming.

1924 Sylvia opens café with Corio at the Red Cottage,
Woodford.

1926 Christabel and Emmeline Pankhurst return to London.

1927 Emmeline Pankhurst becomes Conservative candidate for
Whitechapel but fails to win the seat. Sylvia gives birth
to a son, Richard Keir Pethick Pankhurst.

1928 Emmeline Pankhurst dies. Act passed to give women full
adult suffrage.

1931 Sylvia's book *The Suffragette Movement* published.

1932   Sylvia's book on the war, *The Home Front*, published.

1936   Mussolini invades Abyssinia (Ethiopia). Sylvia espouses Ethiopian cause. Christabel made Dame Commander of British Empire.

1939   Second World War breaks out. Sylvia supports it as war against Fascism. Christabel settles in America.

1950   Death of Corio. Sylvia settles in Ethiopia.

1958   Christabel dies in Santa Monica.

1959   Christabel's book *Unshackled* published posthumously.

1960   Sylvia dies in Addis Ababa. Emperor Haile Selassie attends her funeral.

To my great-niece, Rachel

ONE

Childhood

In 1890 two little girls played happily together in the garden of Russell Square, London, on which their comfortable home abutted. Christabel, aged ten, was the pretty one. Sylvia, aged eight, was plain, but was already showing an artist's sensitivity to her surroundings. She was to describe their childhood in detail in her autobiography, *The Suffragette Movement*, published forty-one years later. 'Christabel', she wrote,

was our mother's favourite: we all knew it and I for one never resented it. It was a matter of course: and I loved her too much to be jealous of her. It was a joy to me to walk beside her, half a step in arrear, gazing upon the delicate pink and white of her face and neck, contrasted against the young, green plants coming up in the square garden in the Spring. She was tenacious of her position as the eldest and the favourite, but she exercised it on the whole without offence.

So close were the sisters that Sylvia could only remember one childhood quarrel between them and that one so 'brief' and 'slight' that she could not remember the cause, but only how she stood in the dusk on the landing outside the nursery in abject misery until Christabel took her into her arms again. The arrival of a younger sister, Adela, and two brothers, Harry and Frank (who died young), had not broken their intimacy.

There was nothing then to indicate the bitter rift that was to divide the two sisters in later years, when they disagreed over the tactics of the women's suffrage campaign and indeed developed wholly divergent philosophies of struggle, philosophies that were to represent the two strands of the development of feminism.

'Mother' was Emmeline Pankhurst, later to become the legendary founder of the Suffragettes. Beautiful, elegant and romantic, she seemed at first sight an unlikely candidate for protest and prison. As the daughter of Robert Goulden, a self-made wealthy cotton manufacturer, she was comfortably reared in their home on the outskirts of Manchester. She received the usual sketchy education of a Victorian girl, to which she added her own passion for reading, which she passed on to her children. A lively and precocious child, she was the apple of her father's eye. He even sent her to finish her education in Paris, where she acquired her taste for elegance and became a close friend of Noémie de Rochefort, daughter of the Marquis de Rochefort-Luçay, who, as a Communist, refused to use his title and was nearly executed for his part in the Paris Commune of the 1870s. Henri de Rochefort became a romantic revolutionary hero to the young Emmeline, but this did not prevent her from toying with the idea, which she cooked up with Noémie, of marrying a French man of letters to whom her friend introduced her. The idea was scotched only by her father's flat refusal to provide the necessary dowry.

Like many a self-made Manchester businessman Robert Goulden was a Liberal, and Emmeline grew up amid the progressive ideas that were rife in Manchester. She helped collect money for the emancipated American slaves, and at the age of twelve was taken to women's suffrage meetings by her mother, where she heard Lydia Becker, secretary of the Manchester Women's Suffrage Society, speak. Goulden admired the brilliant radical lawyer Dr Richard Pankhurst, who had become a force in Manchester with his championing of every reforming cause, however unpopular: free secular education, nationalization of the land and of the mines, adult suffrage, the abolition of the House of Lords (which he described as 'the most preposterous institution in Europe') and many others. Goulden supported the doctor enthusiastically in his campaign against Disraeli's aggressively imperialist and expansionist policy.

But when Emmeline came back to Manchester, heard Dr Pankhurst speak and fell in love with him, it was a different story. Emmeline marry him? Ridiculous! Damn it all, the man was a Republican and practically an atheist – to say nothing of being twenty years her senior. But Emmeline discovered a hidden streak of stubbornness within herself. She was intoxicated by Richard Pankhurst's idealism, eloquence – and beautiful white hands. Marry him she would, and did.

Money was tight. Dr Pankhurst's unpopular views had cost him many legal briefs. An indignant Robert Goulden refused to help. Undaunted, Emmeline continued to lay her plans. She wanted to see her adored husband in Parliament. Her ambition for him – and her desire to make him financially independent by opening a fancy-goods business – brought them to London and to No. 8 Russell Square.

Emmeline was now effectively in control. She was never to see her husband in Parliament: he had broken with the

Liberals on a number of issues, including women's suffrage (which Gladstone opposed), and unsuccessfully fought the Manchester by-election as an Independent in 1883. His views were too radical for most of his Liberal allies. Even Lydia Becker refused him the support of her Women's Suffrage Society, maintaining that he was too much of a firebrand. In London he was to fight another unsuccessful election at Rotherhithe.

But Russell Square had political compensations for the frustrated Emmeline. The large double drawing-room on the first floor of No. 8, painted her favourite yellow, become her salon, brightened with unsold bric-à-brac from the fancy-goods shop: Chinese teapots, Japanese embroidery, Indian brasses, William Morris cretonnes. Here Emmeline held her suffrage meetings, poetry readings and musical afternoons. Through here streamed a succession of political thinkers and agitators: socialists, Fabians, anarchists, free thinkers, radicals of every variety; refugees from the Paris Commune; William Morris himself; Tom Mann, the union leader; Annie Besant, brilliant feminist pamphleteer, busy helping to organize the match-girls' strike. The house was alive with the ferment of ideas.

Emmeline presided over her salon with grace and charm. The little girls, normally relegated to the upstairs nursery, were allowed down on social occasions to hand round collecting bags for good causes and enjoy the strawberry teas. Dr Pankhurst was only too glad to give his wife her head as she hung pictures, laid carpets, made curtains and upholstered furniture. 'I am a helpless creature!' he would sigh among his books, even leaving his wife to carve the joint. She also took charge of their children's upbringing, in which she was a strict disciplinarian. She had no use for fads and fancies. The nursery breakfast of porridge had to be eaten, even if it was cold and lumpy. The little girls were often sent over to the Russell Square gardens to play alone.

For an 'avant garde' woman (at one stage she had suggested to Dr Pankhurst that they should forgo the legal formalities of marriage, as it was no institution for free spirits) she had some strange inconsistencies. She rejected their father's plea that the girls should go to school, arguing that they were 'too highly strung' and would 'lose all originality'. Their education was gleaned from the reading of books and from trips to museums with their governess, but above all from the challenge of ideas in which they were brought up. This suited the girls well enough, particularly the shy Sylvia, although when belatedly they had a spell at school, where Sylvia was miserable, Christabel was in her element.

For the sisters were already developing very different characters. Christabel had her mother's social ease and charm, and shared her love of pretty things. She chafed against the economical dresses of navy blue serge, with knickers to match, in which they were clothed. When Emmeline's friend Noémie, now Madame Dufaux, came to stay, bringing them white muslin pinafores trimmed with lace from Paris, Christabel insisted that they wear them as petticoats under their dresses with the lace showing, like other girls. She liked to be in the swim.

Sylvia, though meekly obedient, was indifferent to such frippery. Instead of being happily extrovert like Christabel, she agonized in her private miseries. She did not have Christabel's robust constitution, being prone to attacks of nervous depression of frightening intensity, which she tried to hide. 'I never attempted to draw Christabel, my companion, from the sunny favour of the household into the drear wastes of misery,' she recorded. As a little girl her eyes were weak and she was not encouraged to read, so she was eternally grateful to Christabel, who read to her for hours at a stretch. (Emmeline had a fastidious aversion to spectacles.) Later Sylvia rebelled against the nurserymaid's limp rendering of one of her favourite books and decided to read for herself.

But she lived in a world of her own, peopled by dreams. 'Anything ugly or sordid brought despondency, often re-current and difficult to overcome,' she explained, so she created her own beauty. One of her favourite dreams was of a country house with daisied lawns, a river flowing through the meadows, pigeons cooing in the woods, dappled fawns feeding out of her hand and peacocks on the terraces, which was to be their home one day. (William Morris was always to influence her art.) 'It was a childish fancy,' she mused retrospectively, 'gradually developing and extending to the hope of a commonwealth, where all should be "better than well".' In the meantime sketching and drawing were her great release.

Sylvia was devoted to her mother. She was as dazzled by her beauty as she was by Christabel's prettiness. She would hear nothing against her. One day she overheard a friend of the family, Mrs Blatch, remark to her mother that Sylvia looked delicate. 'She will not eat her porridge,' Mrs Pankhurst replied sternly. 'Then why not give her some-thing else?' retorted Mrs Blatch. What about eggs, fish, bacon, kidneys, fruit? Such treason to her mother shook Sylvia. 'My loyalty rallied to her: was she not the most beautiful woman in the world?' None of the ladies who came to their house could compare with her.

How clear was her beautiful pallor, how finely arched her delicate black eyebrows, how soft and tender her large, violet eyes. She had the loveliness of the moon, and the grace of the slender silver birch. I gazed on her with adoration.

But it was her father who was the great influence in Sylvia's life. 'O splendid father!' she wrote of him. Despite his fiery speeches Dr Pankhurst was a gentle man. 'Love each other!' he constantly admonished not only his children but the world. 'My children are the four pillars of my house,' he told them tenderly. The revolutionary causes he espoused were all part of a benign generosity of spirit. 'If you do not work for other people, you will not have been worth the upbringing,' he urged his children. Privilege and exploitation were to give way to the common weal.

To Sylvia he was the model of all one should aspire to be. She was to devote a long chapter in her autobiography to a eulogy of his public-spirited activities.

Our father, vilified and boycotted, yet beloved by a multitude of people in all walks of life, was a standard bearer of every forlorn hope, every unpopular yet worthy cause then conceived for the uplifting of oppressed and suffering humanity.

She applauded her mother as the most zealous of his disciples.

But there was one particular theme that Sylvia learned from him which she never forgot. To Richard Pankhurst, the fight for women's rights was part of the fight against exploitation everywhere. No society could be just in which the majority of its citizens were political and economic slaves. So he fought for votes for women as instinctively as he fought for votes for workingmen, in order to secure the same educational and economic fulfilment for them both.

Complete adult suffrage, he believed, should be the goal of every socialist.

Progress in extending the franchise even to men had so far been slow. The Reform Bill of 1832, passed three years before Richard Pankhurst was born, had been hailed as a great democratic advance, but, in fact, its scope was very limited. True, it abolished the rotten and pocket boroughs, proclaiming as its intention 'to deprive many inconsiderable Places of the Right of returning Members, to grant such Privilege to large, populous and wealthy Towns, to increase the Number of Knights of the Shire, to extend the Elective Franchise to many of His Majesty's Subjects who have not hitherto enjoyed the same'. But it gave the vote merely to the occupiers, as owners or tenants, of property of the 'clear yearly value' of £10 – a considerable sum in those days – with a still higher property qualification for tenants in the counties, which meant that only one in seven of the adult male population of the United Kingdom was enfranchised. The workingmen of the 'populous and wealthy Towns', like Manchester and Birmingham, were still ignored. As far as women were concerned, the Act of 1832 actually made matters worse. By assigning the vote to 'every male person of full age' who qualified, it employed the term 'male person' for the first time in English law. Women property owners were by definition non-persons. Despite the insult, women had been slow to move. They grumbled, but they did not act. They were trapped in the Victorian concept of their role, epitomized by Tennyson's lines in 'The Princess':

> Man with the head and woman with the heart;
> Man to command and woman to obey.

But by 1867 women had begun to stir themselves. The

Representation of the People Bill of that year, by extending the vote to 'every man' who was a ratepaying householder and to the better-off male lodgers in the towns, heightened the discrimination against women and made it less bearable. For the first time the women's point of view was pressed in Parliament when John Stuart Mill, the bold champion of women's rights, moved an amendment to the Bill to substitute the word 'person' for 'man' thus enfranchising women. The women's spirits rose as he managed to rally 74 votes to his opponents' 197. Women's suffrage societies started to spring up, with Manchester, home of radical causes, in the lead. When in 1867 a society for the promotion of women's suffrage was formed in Manchester, Richard Pankhurst was one of its originators. Lydia Becker, the formidable driving force behind the new women's campaign, became its general secretary. She used the dedicated Dr Pankhurst mercilessly, bombarding him with letters. 'Miss Bancroft of St Anne's Manor,' she wrote to him in 1868, 'is intensely indignant at having no vote. Three of her employees – men who live in small cottages – have votes and she who pays so large a rent and rates and keeps the three men at work cannot have one. "It is infamous," she says.'

Thus urged on, Dr Pankhurst threw his legal expertise into the fray, trying unsuccessfully to convince the Board of Overseers in Manchester that the Act, by using the word 'man', had by inference enfranchised women. In good law, he argued, 'man' was the equivalent of the Latin *homo* and *homo*, far from meaning 'man' in contradistinction to 'woman', meant 'human being'. It was a good try. Using the same argument, a few women even managed to get on the voting list in one or two areas and it took a court ruling to strike them off.

Women were asserting themselves at last and the next twenty years saw an outburst of Parliamentary activity on their behalf. Gradually some concessions were won. Married women were given the right to own their own property in the Married Women's Property Acts of 1870 and 1882. Mothers were given the right to the custody of their children in the Custody of Infants Act of 1886. The Education Act of 1870 gave women the right to vote for, and be elected to, the newly created school boards. In 1869 women had actually won the municipal vote in an amendment to the Municipal Corporations Bill drafted by Dr Pankhurst and fed to Parliamentary supporters. Another important breakthrough was made in 1894, when married women were given the right to all local franchises and became eligible for election as parish and district councillors, as well as Poor Law Guardians.

But the Parliamentary vote still eluded the suffragists, despite the activities of the chain of local women's suffrage societies which had been formed. Under Lydia Becker's dynamic leadership, they worked tirelessly inside and outside the House of Commons to rouse support for the cause, holding meetings, organizing petitions and writing letters to M Ps. But it was all very middleclass, correct and ladylike, and did not make much impact. The women were 'constitutionalists', mainly Liberals, pinning their hopes on converting M Ps and, above all, on Liberal governments. It was disheartening work. Despite the Manchester society's proud title, The Manchester National Society for Women's Suffrage, the women's movement was decentralized and fragmented. To combat this, Lydia Becker persuaded the local societies to form a central committee to work with the Parliamentary Committee for Women's Suffrage which had been set up by sympathetic MPs, but the women were soon shown their place. They were not allowed to attend the MPs' committee and had to wait outside the door while the men conferred. The supreme insult came in 1884 when another Representation of the People Act extended the household and lodger franchise to the countryside and gave the vote to agricultural labourers in their tied cottages, but still left women out. A sardonic amendment promoted by Lord John Manners to enable a woman farmer to appoint a manservant to vote on her behalf failed to move Gladstone. The death of Lydia Becker in 1890 was the final blow. The way forward seemed barred. And over all towered Queen Victoria with her implacable hostility to this 'mad folly of Women's Rights'.

Two strands of thought were therefore emerging in the Pankhurst women's minds. They were becoming socialists, but they were also becoming more assertively feminist. In 1893 the family returned to Manchester. Emmeline's business had been a flop and the money had run out. They were to find their consolation in intense political activity.

British politics were in a state of flux. Up till the 1890s working-class men seeking to redress their grievances had voted Liberal. New shoots of working-class independence through socialism were beginning to appear. In 1881 the Democratic Federation, which three years later was to become the Social Democratic Federation (SDF), had been formed; this was followed by the Fabian Society in 1884. Though small in influence, both were to help sow the seed of the revolutionary idea that if working people were to be properly represented, they must represent themselves. This independent socialist approach was bolstered up by the growth of trade unions and the emergence of Robert

Owen's Co-operative movement as an expression of working-class self-help. Radical societies of various kinds were growing up everywhere.

This development was very much to the liking of Richard and Emmeline Pankhurst. And when in 1892 a portent of this new working-class assertion of independence burst upon the House of Commons in the form of Keir Hardie, the first independent working-class M P, they were ready and eager to become his devotees. Emmeline Pankhurst, in fact, was later to catch the 'independent representation' principle from him. If working-class people must have their own independent movement in order to achieve their aims, should this not apply to women as well?

Keir Hardie's election to Parliament electrified the Liberal and Conservative establishments. Born in Lanarkshire in 1856, the illegitimate son of Mary Kerr, a farm servant who was later to marry David Hardie, a ship's carpenter, he had started work at eight as an errand-boy and grown up in grinding poverty. His later work in the pits had brought him into the trade-union movement and he had unsuccessfully fought a by-election in Lanarkshire in 1888 as the miners' candidate. His election for West Ham in 1892 as candidate of the Radical Association was in no small part due to the unexpected death of the official Liberal candidate, leaving him with a straight fight against the Conservatives. Nonetheless his arrival in the House of Commons, dressed in cloth cap and tweeds, leaving a wife and children at home in Lanarkshire, marked a turning point in British politics. Despite catcalls and jeers at his unconventional garb, he remained defiantly his own man, announcing his intention to sit on the opposition benches, whatever government, Liberal or Conservative, was in power. A new era had begun.

A year later Keir Hardie, who had already helped to launch the Scottish Labour Party, now helped to found the Independent Labour Party (ILP) in Bradford, a move that was eventually to give birth to the Labour Party nationally. The intrepid Richard and Emmeline were among the first to join the ILP, which brought Dr Pankhurst more public odium and cost him more legal briefs. Christabel was to write of him proudly in her autobiography, *Unshackled: The Story of How We Won the Vote*, published after her death:

But he could never lag behind his conviction. He nailed his colours to the mast. Gallant as ever, he held his head high and faced the new storm that broke upon him as the first man of his sort and standing in the city, perhaps in the whole country, to join the Labour movement.

When in 1895 he fought the Gorton by-election for the ILP, the girls once again experienced the bitterness of political defeat and the shock of their mother being stoned by roughs who were celebrating the Tory victory with free drinks.

In all this tumult the girls were learning social and political history almost without knowing it. They had participated in their father's electoral campaign and were to get a new eye-opener when their mother, taking advantage of the 1894 Act, was elected to the Chorlton Board of Guardians. In an age without social insurance or social security the horrors of destitution were borne in on her. When unemployment reached record heights in the winter of 1894/5 Mrs Pankhurst was told the guardians could not give relief to the 'able-bodied poor'. Her response was to organize food kitchens with the help of the ILP. Sylvia spent her Saturdays traipsing round with her mother, distributing mugs of soup and loaves of bread to the hungry workless shivering in the bitter cold.

Conditions in the workhouses horrified Emmeline. With her husband's help she launched a campaign for the reform of the Poor Law and managed to get abandoned children out of the workhouse and into cottage homes. The callous treatment of young women left with illegitimate babies angered her. 'Though I had been a suffragist before,' she wrote a few years later, 'I now began to think about the vote in women's hands not only as a right, but as a desperate necessity.'

All this was good training for the Suffragette agitation that was to come, and the two sisters, now plugging one of the gaps in their education at Manchester High School, drank it all in. Their best lesson in agitation came from the incident at Boggart Clough, a large, municipally owned open space which the ILP had used for its meetings for several years. In 1896 a hostile Parks Committee decided to ban its use by the ILP. Floods of speakers defied the ban. Fines were imposed on speakers, collectors and literature sellers. Many refused to pay the fine. Some were sent to gaol. Audiences grew from hundreds to thousands as the battle went on. Mrs Pankhurst, collecting at one of the meetings, was summoned before the bench. The magistrates were astonished to find before them the wife of a senior member of the Bar. 'She stood there,' wrote Sylvia, 'looking entirely well at ease and self-possessed, wearing an elegant little bonnet of pink straw, her slender, black-gloved hands lying quietly on the rail of the dock before her.' Firmly, she told the magistrates that she would pay no fine and would return to the meetings as long as she was at large. Nonetheless the case against her was dismissed. Angry at this discrimination in her favour when others were imprisoned, she went to the Clough Sunday after Sunday to take the chair on the makeshift platform which the ILP had erected in the park for its open-air meetings, losing her old nervousness. As always, even under the stress of public speaking, she remained elegant. Sylvia recalled: 'The little pink bonnet she had worn in the dock was the rallying centre to which all eyes turned. So popular it grew that again and again, as it faded, she made it anew with fresh straw.' Eventually the ban was withdrawn. Courage and agitation had won the day. It was a lesson the girls did not forget.

At this time a new formative influence came into Sylvia's life. The great Keir Hardie was coming to tea! She described the magical moment in *Myself When Young*:

I hastened from school. He was in the big armchair, a sturdy figure in a rough, brown homespun jacket, with a majestic head, the brow massive, the gold-brown eyes deep-set. Venerable age, vigorous youth seemed blended in him. The strength of a rock, the ruggedness of a Scotch moorland, the sheltering kindness of an oak, the gentleness of a great St Bernard dog – these similes float through the mind at the thought of him.

At forty years old he was everything her young being craved for: a father figure who could be more than a father to her. He became the great love of her life at a time when another love was to be taken from her.

For some time Richard Pankhurst's health had been far from good. Sylvia had noted with anxiety his increasing attacks of pain, which he brushed aside. Worn down with money worries and the constant campaigning on which he spent himself, he had developed an ulcer, though his family was unaware of it. In 1898 Emmeline took Christabel to stay with Noémie Dufaux, now in Geneva, to perfect her French. Sylvia, left at home to look after her father, became alarmed when she found him doubled in agony, but her pleas to be allowed to bring Emmeline home were rejected. At last he agreed that his wife should be summoned, but when she arrived the ulcer had perforated and he was dead. The two women clung to each other in a paroxysm of grief.

TWO

Suffragettes

Richard Pankhurst had left his family no money: he had
none to leave. ILP friends wanted to set up a fund for the
education of his children, but proud Mrs Pankhurst would
have none of it. Ironically, their father had always said to
his children, 'What do you want to be when you grow up?
Get something to work at that you like and can do.' But
when it came to it, they were left without any trained skills
at all. Emmeline had seen to that. At one stage Christabel
had shown a flair for dancing and her mother had played
with the idea that Christabel would become a ballet dancer
and that she would accompany her on world tours. That
dream died quite rapidly. Another idea with which
Christabel toyed was that she would take up dressmaking,
but her mother was in one of her moods in which she
distrusted the professions. That idea died too.

Sylvia was luckier. She had her painting and sketching,
which had kept her happy during a childhood in which her
health and eyesight – to say nothing of her sociability – had
not been good. Just before her father died it had been
arranged, to her great delight, that she would take lessons
from a well-known artist, and the house was full of her
drawings. Following Richard Pankhurst's death, the

furniture of their home had to be sold preparatory to their moving to a smaller house. A friend, Charles Rowley, came to assess the value of some old paintings they possessed, saw Sylvia's drawings and sent some of them to the Manchester School of Art. The result was the award of a free studentship. Curiously, her artistic skill was a few years later to be the launching pad of the Suffragettes.

Her zest for life gone, Mrs Pankhurst had to earn a living. The Chorlton Board of Guardians, impressed by her record of work with them and touched by her tragedy, offered her a registrarship of births and deaths and she accepted it. At least it was an income which enabled her to afford the smaller house in Nelson Street, Manchester, to which they moved. But she still hankered after the idea of opening a shop, despite the failure of her previous efforts in this direction. This new effort was also to prove a white elephant.

A listless Christabel was brought back from Geneva to help with her mother's shop. She came dutifully, but she hated it. 'Business was not good for me and I was not good for business,' she wrote later. Home life was very changed. 'All was now in the minor key, depressed, forlorn.' So were her prospects. Her lively mind had never been disciplined. She was at a loose end. Even her adoring mother said she had 'no particular bent'.

But breakthroughs were to come for both girls. Sylvia found hers through the Art School. 'In spite of our grief and my nervous depression, when absorbed in the work I knew the greatest happiness,' she wrote in her autobiography. Her studiousness was rewarded with a travelling scholarship and she selected Venice, where she wanted to study mosaics. It was, she recalled, 'the promised land of my sad young heart, craving for beauty, fleeing from the sorrowful ugliness of factory-ridden Lancashire, and the dull, aching poverty of its slums; Venice, O city of dreaming magic!' She was determined to make use of every minute, rising at five, painting till breakfast, then visiting churches to copy the mosaics, then more painting till darkness came. She was intoxicated with it all. Crowds gathered round her as she painted outdoors as long as the light lasted. She was not put off even when some young girls pronounced her '*brutta*' (plain-looking) and the women replied, '*Sì, sì, ma simpatica.*' It seemed then as though her art was to become her life.

Typically, Christabel stumbled on her breakthrough almost by accident. To rouse her out of lethargy, her mother persuaded her to take some lecture courses at Manchester University. One afternoon she attended a lecture on the poets and politics. It was followed by a discussion. She had not had, she recalled, the faintest intention of saying a word. 'Yet, to my own surprise, the discourse and the debate stirred a thought in me and the thought would out. I rose and rather nervously uttered a sentence or two.' 'Who is that?' the Vice-Chancellor asked the graduate sitting next to him and made a flattering reference to her contribution in his winding-up remarks. Without knowing it she was launched on a career.

In the audience were two go-ahead women's vote activists, Eva Gore-Booth and Esther Roper, who were seeking to revive the flagging fortunes of the women's cause. Following Lydia Becker's death nine years earlier, the local newly emerging women's suffrage societies had become divided in their aims, uncertain whether to embroil themselves with political parties or to remain politically neutral.

The extension of the male franchise in 1884 had given a fillip to the organization of politics, and therefore of women, on party lines and had diverted much female talent and energy into bodies like the Women's Liberal Unionist Association. In 1888 the suffrage societies had actually split over the question of whether the Women's Liberal Federation should be allowed to affiliate to them. It was a classic dilemma that was to repeat itself.

Another problem was that Lydia's death had deprived the cause of dynamic leadership. Lydia's successor, Mrs Millicent Fawcett, was of a very different ilk. Her abilities were undoubted, but she lacked Becker's driving force. Daughter of Newson Garrett, a staunch feminist, she was instinctively a feminist herself, but she had wider interests than getting women the vote. She wrote works on political economy, published two novels, founded Newnham College, campaigned for the Married Women's Property Act and acted as secretary to her husband, Henry Fawcett, the blind Liberal MP. It was not until he died in 1884 that she turned her attention to the suffrage campaign, working closely with Lydia Becker until her death. Her biggest contribution as Lydia's successor was to draw the divided societies together again and to help form the National Union of Women's Suffrage Societies (NUWSS) in 1897.

But she was no firebrand. Leslie Parker Hume, in his history of the NUWSS, described her as 'in many ways a colourless and aloof figure whose rational, calm, understated exterior concealed a remarkable intellect'. Her strength, he wrote, lay in the fact that she embodied the Victorian ideal of womanhood, being 'a model wife and mother and therefore solid and respectable', and did not alienate public opinion as did the 'shrieking sisterhood' of more strident feminists. Her weakness lay in her 'naïve confidence in the innate good sense of the members of Parliament' and her grave underestimation of the toughness of the struggle that lay ahead.

By 1903 the suffrage movement had begun to stir itself again. The Boer War was over and Parliament could turn its mind to other things. The local suffrage societies became more active. The Manchester Society, now the North of England Society, had come under the leadership of Eva Gore-Booth, daughter of an Irish landowner and sister of Countess Markievicz who was later to become the first woman to be elected to Parliament. Eva teamed up with a fellow spirit, Esther Roper, a graduate of Victoria University, who was active in the women's cause. They were both members of the Executive of the NUWSS and together they set out to break down its image as 'a fad of the rich and well-to-do'. They saw votes for women, not just as the 'natural right' on which the Liberals liked to harp, but as a weapon of expediency, essential for the improvement of the conditions of working-class women. Eva was a member of the Manchester Women's Trades Council and she and Esther started a crusade to enthuse the women factory workers of the North, notably in the textile unions, where the women members outnumbered the men. In return they tried to bring the political demands of working women to the attention of Parliament.

Christabel's brave intervention at the lecture caught the attention of the two women. Here, surely, was someone they could use in their campaign. After the meeting they approached her to ask if she would be interested in taking part in their work. Immensely flattered, Christabel jumped at it. Someone wanted her at last! Before she knew where

she was, she was drawn into a round of committee meetings of the NUWSS and of public meetings, indoors and
outdoors, around Manchester. 'Here, then, was an aim in
life for me – the liberation of politically fettered womanhood.'

According to Sylvia, Mrs Pankhurst was intensely jealous
of Christabel's new friends. Partly not to lose her daughter
to them and partly because Christabel's interest in the
women's suffrage movement had rekindled her own, she
gave up her business and concentrated on her registrarship
as well as the women's cause. A remarkable mother-and-
daughter partnership was born.

Christabel was on her way. Nothing could stop her now.
She discovered that she could charm audiences with her
good looks, her quick mind and her vitality. She had found
a role in which she could employ her assets to the full and
in which her less endearing traits could be indulged with
impunity, notably her love of dominance: what Sylvia called
her tendency to be 'tenacious of her position'.

Christabel found to her own surprise that she was a
natural leader and orator. She began to make a name for
herself. The role suited her too, because it brought her into
socially agreeable company. As her father's daughter she
needed a noble cause, but she had never been as emotionally
moved as Sylvia had been by the appalling social conditions
in the slums of Manchester. When they were attending
Manchester High School, Sylvia had noted disapprovingly
how she had developed what Sylvia considered worldly
traits, striking up a friendship with a pretty girl, whom
Sylvia refers to as Edith G—, and comparing her own home
disparagingly with her friend's. At Edith's there appeared to
be a constant round of visits and entertainments, while at

the Pankhursts', according to Christabel, there was 'nothing but politics and silly old women's suffrage'.

It was probably, therefore, as a strategist rather than as a socialist that Christabel accepted the need, urged by her two friends, to increase the impact of the suffrage campaign by involving the working-class women in the textile towns around Manchester. She certainly knew how to appeal to working-class audiences, particularly the women textile workers who were well organized and relatively better off than many of their depressed sisters. It was at one of her innumerable meetings that her eloquence so roused an Oldham mill girl, Annie Kenney, that she threw up her job and became a suffrage campaign organizer, living like a daughter in the Pankhurst home. She was to be a useful proletarian leaven in a movement which was to remain firmly − and to Christabel rightly − in middle-class hands and to attract a wide following of wealthy, socially eminent and sometimes titled women.

In the event, it was Sylvia, immersed as she was in her art, who precipitated the incident that was to mould history. Back from Venice to a life of painting and housekeeping, she was asked by the ILP to decorate a hall it had erected in Salford to her father's memory. She gladly took on the task and slaved night and day for three months − without pay − to complete the work on time. When it was due to be opened, she learned to her astonishment that women were not to be allowed to use the Pankhurst Hall because it had a men-only social club attached to it. The irony of the insult inflamed the Pankhurst family. An indignant Emmeline Pankhurst declared it was clear that men would never liberate women, and that the ILP men were no better than any other in this respect. Women must liberate themselves.

She called a few ILP women to her home in Nelson Street, and then and there formed the Women's Social and Political Union (WSPU) with the stirring motto: 'Deeds, Not Words'. For eleven years it was to be the vehicle for her and Christabel's views.

While her mother and sister were launching the WSPU on its defiant course, Sylvia was in London, having won a scholarship to the Royal College of Art in South Kensington. Although she was 'horribly lonely' in her lodgings off the Fulham Road, she nonetheless felt herself 'one of the privileged of the world' in being able to devote herself to 'the study and creation of beauty'. She also had other consolations. Her beloved brother Harry was in school in Hampstead and they spent alternate Sundays together. Also her friendship with Keir Hardie was deepening. She was a frequent visitor to his London lodgings in Neville Court, where he lived frugally in one large room divided by a curtain, making his own simple meals. She loved to sit by the fire with him, where they were sometimes joined by Harry, while he toasted scones and reminisced about the hardships of his life as a child and later as a miner, or read aloud from his wide range of books before turning back to the pile of work waiting for him as an MP.

Her relationship with Keir Hardie fused together all the strands of her aching personality: the need for a father figure, hunger for love, hatred of injustice and a strong sense of social guilt. Obsessed though she was with her art, her conscience would not let her neglect her political activities. She joined the Fulham branch of the ILP and when her mother, in her new role as stirrer-up-in-chief of the women's suffrage campaign, descended on her from Manchester for help in her activities, she was always ready to drop everything to do her bidding. The two rooms in Park Walk, Chelsea, to which she moved, became the *pied-à-terre* for a stream of WSPU visitors – particularly her mother and Annie Kenney – and the base from which the London committee of the WSPU was launched. 'There were no more Saturday painting parties at Park Walk after that,' noted Sylvia sadly. 'My life was changed.'

The irreverent tactics of the Pankhursts, challenging every politician within sight, had already caused a stir. Not everyone approved of them. Millicent Fawcett's NUWSS preferred to rely on its friends in Parliament to do their best for it, and session after session had been allowed to pass without the introduction of a Bill for women's suffrage. When the new session opened in 1905, Emmeline vowed that this time it would be different. She came up to London to lobby MPs, sweeping Sylvia along with her.

For hour after hour the two women lobbied alone, with only Keir Hardie to comfort them. The MPs' ballot for the right to introduce a Bill of their own, known as a Private Member's Bill, which was held at the beginning of each session, was about to take place and they pleaded with a succession of MPs to give a place in the ballot to the women's cause. The only firm pledge they got was from Keir Hardie himself and, when he was unsuccessful, Emmeline was in despair. He rallied her by suggesting she might persuade a successful MP to take on the cause. Bamford Slack, who had won fourteenth place in the ballot and therefore had a good chance of introducing a Bill, seemed a likely prospect. Frantic telephoning followed and Emmeline finally cornered Slack in his own home. He hesitated, but eventually capitulated 'at the request of his wife', according to Sylvia. The debate was fixed for 12 May 1905.

Emmeline's spirits now soared again. Victory, she was sure, was in their grasp. This session would see the cause triumphant. Other women's societies now caught the excitement. A petition was organized, meetings held all over London, with Sylvia's modest budget drained by the bus fares to get to them. The N U W S S held a meeting of support in the Queen's Hall. Fifty M Ps (all in evening dress, sniffed Sylvia) were on the platform and testified their support in a few trite words. Millicent Fawcett, 'a trim, prim little figure', made a speech in a 'clear, pleasant voice'. Other women speakers nervously added their quota. 'It was all very polite and very tame; different indeed from the rousing Socialist meetings of the North, to which I was accustomed,' wrote Sylvia scathingly.

On 12 May women crowded into the lobby, overflowing it. Some had even come from Australia. They were in high spirits, anticipating victory. But inside the chamber a farce was being played. The first Order of the Day was an insignificant little measure which could have been dispatched in an hour, but this did not stop the filibusterers. They played out time, barely troubling to hide their jocularity. When Bamford Slack's turn came, there was a mere half hour left. Suddenly the women outside realized what had happened: their Bill had not been defeated, it had simply been contemptuously talked out. Excitedly the women gathered at a spot near the House and held an indignant meeting. Angrily, they passed a resolution condemning the Government. But the catastrophe played into the Pankhursts' hands. It showed, they argued, that the Fawcett tactic of relying on Private Members' Bills was a waste of time. The Government must legislate and they must give it no peace until it did.

Two months later Arthur Balfour's Government was to prove their point. With unemployment rising, the King's Speech had promised a Bill to help the unemployed by finding them work on farm colonies. Keir Hardie led the campaign for the Bill in Parliament. A thousand destitute workless marched to Westminster from the East End. But Balfour's backbenchers were up in arms at the Bill's alleged profligacy and the Prime Minister announced that it would be postponed. Angry mobs of unemployed took to the streets in Manchester and four men were arrested in the disturbances. A frightened Government backed down again and ten days later the Bill became law.

The lesson was not lost on the WSPU; the threat of violence had done the trick. 'It was only a question now as to how militant tactics would begin,' commented Sylvia.

Christabel had no doubts as to what should be done. Within the space of a few weeks the 'family party' of the Pankhursts, as its critics sneeringly called it, had put itself at the head of a nationwide militant movement, and in Manchester she was busy equipping herself to lead the fray. Esther Roper, impressed by Christabel's skill in argument, suggested to her mother that she ought to study law. A gratified Emmeline approached Lord Haldane, an avowed supporter of women's rights, asking him to sponsor Christabel as a student at Lincoln's Inn, where her father had studied before her. Lord Haldane readily agreed, but the application was summarily dismissed on the grounds, among others, that there would be no point in admitting her, as women were not allowed to practise at the Bar anyway. The propaganda point was not lost on the fair-minded and when later Christabel and another rejected applicant, Miss Cave, were invited to address the Union

Society in London, they easily persuaded the assembled lawyers to carry a motion in favour of women being admitted to their profession. But Christabel was getting tired of scoring propaganda points that led nowhere. 'That did not open the doors closed against us,' she noted tersely.

Not to be deterred, she enrolled at Manchester University for a three-year course leading to a law degree. Somehow she managed to fit her studies into the mounting volume of her suffrage work. As Annie Kenney put it, 'Where she studied, how she studied is a mystery. She was working for the movement the whole of the day and practically every night.' Christabel herself admitted that, as her final examination approached, 'panic prompted concentration and I withdrew from human society to that of my books'. Her quick mind and retentive memory saved the day; the cramming worked and she graduated with first-class honours in June 1906. The training was to give her confidence in her battles with the courts.

But she was also steadily evolving her political strategy. Sentiment and loyalty to her father's ideals had no part in it. Coolly and calculatingly (Sylvia and their younger sister, Adela, would have said cold-bloodedly) she fixed her eyes on one all-consuming aim: to get women the vote. Social reform must wait. Indeed, under her influence the WSPU line was to reject any reforming legislation, however laudable, which women had had no part in framing. The winning of the sex war must have overriding priority.

This approach led logically to the breaking of party ties. She and her mother were still active members of the ILP and her mother had been elected to its National Administrative Committee, but in her mind Christabel was increasingly moving away from it. The setting up of a small independent Labour Group of MPs, an historic step towards the formation of the Parliamentary Labour Party, left her cold. Keir Hardie was a dear friend and ally, of course, who stood by the WSPU through thick and thin, but even he would have to be sacrificed, if and when necessary. In the meantime she used him to put her ideas across in the *Labour Leader*, of which he was editor. He published a letter from her in which she fulminated against the failure of a recent Labour conference to condemn women's vote-lessness. 'Apparently delegates will be satisfied with the presence in the House of Commons of a "Labour Group" over which working women have no control,' she stormed.

It will be said, perhaps, that the interests of women will be safe in the hands of the men's Labour Party. Never in the history of the world have the interests of those without power to defend themselves been properly served by others.

She followed it up with another attack. 'Why are women expected to have such confidence in the men of the Labour Party? Working men are as unjust to women as are those of other classes.'

These were fighting words but, in her pursuit of sex equality at the expense of other equalities, Christabel was ready to lower her sights. In its inaugural leaflet the WSPU had defined its aim as being to ensure that 'for all purposes connected with, and having reference to, the right to vote at Parliamentary elections, words in the Representation of the People Act importing the masculine gender shall include women'. In less legal jargon the WSPU was prepared to accept for women any franchise that might be currently approved for men by Parliament. Sensing she was on rather illogical ground, which would still leave millions of women

45

disfranchised, Christabel spelt out her justification in a pamphlet, *The Citizenship of Women: A Plea for Women's Suffrage*, which she persuaded Keir Hardie to get the ILP to publish. In it she pleaded that it was hard enough to get support for a limited measure giving women the existing property-based vote. How much harder it would be to get them included in a wider franchise.

> The man, even if he be of the working classes, will not lightly or all at once part with the authority which has so long been his and admit that the wife of his bosom is his political equal. But once some women become voters, the male mind will insensibly accustom itself to the idea of women's citizenship and the way be thus prepared for adult suffrage unrestricted by sex, poverty or marriage.

It was gradualism with a vengeance.

To the newly emerging Labour Party such an approach was anathema. It believed, as Richard Pankhurst had done, that the fight for women's rights was part of the battle for all disfranchised groups, notably the working-class men and women they were in business to represent. Christabel had claimed that a limited measure would 'at once lift 1,250,000 women from the political sphere to which idiots, lunatics and paupers are consigned', but these would by definition be women of property – the very ones likely to oppose the extension of the franchise to the lower orders. So the aim must be adult suffrage at one blow. Christabel's line was also alien to Sylvia and Adela, but Christabel accepted a rift with them with equanimity. It was she and her mother who determined WSPU policy.

Her job now was to put the WSPU on the map. It had started well, but it desperately needed publicity. Propaganda meetings were all very well, but they did not hit the head-lines. What was needed was a sustained campaign to harass the Government. Its candidates must be opposed at every election, its ministers heckled wherever they spoke, deputations and demonstrations organized. And Christabel herself must give the lead.

Her first attempt was nervously ladylike. In 1904 the Liberal Party was girding its loins for the general election that could not be far away and in which it was confident of defeating Balfour's Conservative Government. Its battle cry was free trade and Winston Churchill was due to launch the campaign in a major meeting at the Free Trade Hall, Manchester. Christabel applied for a ticket and was given one on the platform. A resolution supporting free trade was moved and, the speeches over, she rose to ask if she could move an amendment on women's suffrage. Politely but firmly the chairman regretted he could not accept it. Amid cries of 'Chair!' from the outraged audience she eventually retired.

She recalled her feelings later:

This was the first militant step – the hardest to me because it *was* the first. To move from my place on the platform to the speaker's table in the teeth of the astonishment and opposition of will of that immense throng, those civic and county leaders and those Members of Parliament, was the most difficult thing I have ever done.

But, she added grimly, it was 'a protest of which little was heard and nothing remembered – because it did not result in imprisonment!' The moral was obvious. She must go to prison. Militancy must have its martyrs. Another time she would not retire so gracefully.

Her next opportunity came a year later when Manchester was again to be the venue for a major Liberal Party rally in the Free Trade Hall. 'Here was my chance!' she wrote in her autobiography. 'I would make amends for my weakness in not pressing that earlier amendment! Now there would be an act the effect of which would remain, a protest not of word, but of deed. Prison this time!' She and Annie prepared the ground carefully. That afternoon they painted a slogan on a huge square of calico to reinforce the verbal questions they intended to ask. 'How should we word it?' they asked themselves.

'Will you give woman suffrage?' – we rejected that form, for the word 'suffrage' suggested to some unlettered or jesting folk the idea of suffering. 'Let them suffer away!' – we had heard the taunt. We must find another wording and we did! It was so obvious and, yet, strange to say, quite new. Our banner bore this terse device WILL YOU GIVE VOTES FOR WOMEN? Thus was uttered for the first time the famous and victorious battle-cry: VOTES FOR WOMEN!

Thus armed, Christabel and Annie sallied forth. '"We shall sleep in prison tonight", said I to Mother. Her face was drawn and cold when I said goodbye.' The hall was crowded, the Liberal audience excited with the prospect of electoral victory. Came question time and Annie Kenney was the first to leap up: 'Will the Liberal Government give votes for women?' No answer. Christabel followed her. The banner was unfurled. The Chief Constable of Manchester approached them, genial and paternal, and promised them their question would be answered after the vote of thanks. They handed it in writing and waited for the reply. Sir Edward Grey rose to reply: their question was ignored. They erupted again. 'Throw them out!' chanted the audience. Stewards rushed at them to drag them from the hall. They were scratched and bruised, but Christabel knew that they had not yet done enough to assure arrest. She must assault the police. How to do it with her arms pinned behind her back? 'Lectures on the law flashed to my mind. I could, even with all my limbs helpless, commit a technical assault and so I found myself arrested and charged with "spitting at a policeman".' The descent into such vulgarity strained her ladylike instincts. 'It was not a real spit,' she insisted in her account of the incident, 'but only, shall we call it, a "pout", a perfectly dry purse of the mouth. I could not *really* have done it, even to get the vote, I think.'

The benign magistrate, who had known her father, was as gentle with them as possible, but to prison they went; Christabel for seven days and Annie for three. They resolutely refused bail or to have their fines paid for them. A fastidious Christabel found prison conditions intensely disagreeable, but her ordeal did not last long. She and Annie returned to a triumphal welcome-back meeting at the Free Trade Hall, a rendezvous especially chosen for the purpose of irony.

The trick worked. There was publicity all right, though by no means all complimentary. 'Strangely enough,' Christabel recorded, 'some who had rallied at the first militant deed thought that this one deed was enough and that militancy should end with its beginning. Representations were made to Mother accordingly.' Ignoring the faint hearts, Christabel merely stepped up her attack. In December 1905 Balfour resigned and the King called on the Liberal leader Henry Campbell-Bannerman to form a government, which he did and promptly went to the country.

This was Christabel's opportunity and she organized her intervention in the general election like a military campaign, issuing a manifesto of women's rights and throwing her troops into the front line of election meetings to create disturbances. The Liberal ministers were her main target, because they were members of a government 'which refuses to give women the vote'.

With women asserting themselves in earnest, masculine chivalry disappeared. Sylvia, brought to the North from London to join in the fray, said the experience was 'like flinging yourself before the hounds in full cry after the fox'. Sent to Sheffield to interrupt a speech by Asquith, then Chancellor of the Exchequer, she and Annie were man-handled by the stewards and men in the audience rained blows on them with fists and umbrellas as they were dragged out. The courage needed to stand up and ask a question had become the courage needed to risk violence.

But Christabel did not lack volunteers. There was plenty of publicity now, and excited women from all ranks of life rallied to the militants. In January 1906 the Liberals swept comfortably back to power – and would obviously be in office for several years. Christabel decided the time had come to invade London. A national movement must have a national base, close to Parliament. Emmeline Pankhurst blanched at the idea. They could not afford it. 'Mother, the money will come,' insisted Christabel. Annie Kenney was dispatched to London to pave the way with £2 in her pocket, all that was left in the election fund.

And the money *did* come, as if by a miracle. News of Christabel's spell in prison had reached South Africa, where two wealthy philanthropic socialists, Frederick and Emmeline Pethick-Lawrence, were on a visit. Intrigued by what they read, they hurried home. They already had a record of good works and left-wing causes behind them, using Frederick's substantial means to found boys' clubs, women's hospitals and university settlements. Frederick had also launched a small monthly paper, the *Labour Record*, which he used to promote the Labour cause. It was soon to be devoted to the cause of the Suffragettes, as the *Daily Mail* had now dubbed the militants. (Christabel thoroughly approved of the new name. The suffragists merely wanted the vote, she explained. The Suffragettes, if you hardened the *g*, stood for 'they mean to get it'.)

Once again it was Keir Hardie who acted as go-between. He gave Mrs Pankhurst an introduction to Mrs Pethick-Lawrence to try to enrol her in the WSPU campaign. The two Emmelines got on well enough, but Mrs Pethick-Lawrence hesitated. 'To tell the truth,' she records in her autobiography,

I had no fancy to be drawn into a small group of brave and reckless and quite helpless people who were prepared to dash themselves against the oldest tradition of human civilization as well as one of the strongest Governments of modern times.

According to her account, it was Annie Kenney – a second emissary from Keir Hardie – who did the trick. Annie's simplicity and wistful eagerness touched her heart: sent from Manchester with £2 in her pocket to 'rouse London'! 'I was amused by Annie's ignorance of what the task of rousing London would involve, and yet thrilled by her courage.' Before she knew where she was, she found herself promising to come along to a committee meeting of the little WSPU band in Sylvia's rooms. The very audacity of the six women gathered there proved irresistible.

I found there was no office, no organization, no money – no postage stamps even ... It was not without dismay that it was borne in on me that somebody had to come to the help of this brave little group and that the finger of fate pointed at me.

By the end of the evening she was joining them in forming the Central London Committee of the WSPU and had agreed to become its honorary treasurer.

Life was now completely transformed for the Suffragettes. Not only did Emmeline Pethick-Lawrence prove to be a brilliant treasurer, getting the accounts properly audited and bubbling with imaginative ideas, but she and her husband placed their house at Clements Inn at the Pankhursts' disposal, retaining only the upstairs flat for their own use and one room as an office for the *Labour Record*. Christabel, hurrying up to London once her law degree was in the bag, was not only given living accommodation there but an office as well. More important still, she was given status. The Pethick-Lawrences treated her like a brilliant daughter, lavishing affection and admiration on her. Emmeline Pethick-Lawrence raved about her charm and oratory, while her husband praised her political skill.

Clements Inn was to become the power-house of the Suffragettes for the next six years. Within a year the WSPU occupied thirteen rooms there. By the end of 1909 it had spread itself into twenty-one rooms. Under Emmeline Pethick-Lawrence's skilful husbandry the money flowed in. Her husband made generous donations. Keir Hardie valiantly raised £300 from ILP sympathizers. Bumper collections were taken at WSPU rallies. Soon the Union had resources that aroused the envy of other suffrage and political groups.

Membership of the WSPU also expanded rapidly. Christabel's leadership seemed to be paying off. Middle-class women flocked to join the cause and Sylvia could understand why. They were aching for 'wider and more important activities and interests'. The universities and a number of professions were now open to them, but prejudice, even among their own parents, held them back. Both branches of the legal profession were still closed to women; the higher teaching and commercial posts were still rigidly confined to men. There was strong prejudice against women doctors. In architecture, engineering and scientific pursuits a woman's breakthrough was so rare that brilliant exceptions like Marie Curie were considered just that: exceptions that did not prove a rule. 'Daughters of rich families were often without personal means,' Sylvia wrote, 'or permitted a meagre dress allowance, and when their parents died, they were often reduced to genteel penury, or unwelcome dependence on relatives.' She commented:

> To many such women, a movement which proclaimed them the equals, nay the superiors of men, demanding for them a worthy position in Society, made an instant appeal, the more so since it offered an outlet from an empty, purposeless existence to an active, exciting part in what it continually insisted to be the most important work in the world.

When women who had led a sheltered life joined with factory workers, shop assistants and teachers to protest against their treatment, she could not stand aside. She understood perfectly how Christabel's campaign made them feel 'persons of consequence'.

Racked with neuralgic pains, Sylvia was agonizing over her problems as usual. She was tormented by a conflict of loyalties: love of her art versus the call to fight for the suffrage cause; loyalty to her father's socialism versus loyalty to her mother in her new crusade. And a new blow was to come. Christabel had long been planning to break with the ILP, and a by-election at Cockermouth brought things to a head. Christabel moved in to pursue her adopted strategy of harrying and attacking the Liberal Government 'at whatever cost'. The local ILP secretary, who put her up, assumed she had come to help the Labour candidate, Robert Smillie, who was in favour of women's suffrage. When instead she set up a rival women's platform and openly incited her audiences to concentrate on defeating the Liberal (which the Conservative candidate did handsomely), her host was, not unnaturally, piqued. Called to account by the ILP's Manchester Central Branch, of which she was a member, she refused to give a pledge that she would not repeat her tactics at future elections. A few months later she resigned from the ILP, taking her mother with her.

To Sylvia the breach between the WSPU and the Labour movement was sacrilege. The return of twenty-nine MPs on the Labour ticket in 1906 seemed to her like the dawn of hope, particularly when Keir Hardie was elected chairman of the new group. She had no illusions about the ambivalent attitude of some of its members towards the militant campaign. Some of the Labour MPs had been elected with the help of Liberal votes. Others believed the small group could be most effective by throwing its weight behind Liberal reforms. A campaign which called on them to oppose the Liberal Government 'at any cost' was repellent. Some, like Philip Snowden, believed the Pankhursts to be self-seeking careerists. Ramsay MacDonald dismissed their 'antics' as disreputable. More members still were not prepared to give women's enfranchisement priority over social issues like the

Right to Work Bill, old-age pensions or the feeding of necessitous schoolchildren, some of the measures the Labour MPs chose for the first ballot for Private Members' Bills in the new Parliament. In urging that women's suffrage should be included in the list, Keir Hardie stood alone. Nevertheless, wrote Sylvia, the Labour Party 'with all its shortcomings, remained throughout the long struggle the only political party willing to declare for women's suffrage'.

The narrowness of Christabel's aims worried her. She felt solidarity with the militants, with her family and with the WSPU that she had helped to form, but was also drawn by the 'poignant, compelling appeal to my heart of the victims of social misery, the white faces in mean streets'. It was the classic dilemma of the feminist movement. Which should have priority: the right to vote or the purposes for which the vote was to be used?

But Christabel was in command. 'A triumvirate was now in supreme control of the Women's Social and Political Union,' she exulted, following her move to Clements Inn. 'To "Mrs Pankhurst and Christabel" was added Mrs Pethick-Lawrence.' But no one doubted who was the boss. Both the Emmelines ceded to Christabel's authority. She cast a spell over them as she did over her audiences. At meetings she would sit quietly at the side of the platform, head down and withdrawn. Then, when her turn came, she would come alive. 'An enthusiast', writing to the *Daily Mail*, was lyrical about her performance in the Peckham by-election. 'Her questioners are for the most part earthenware, and this bit of porcelain does them in the eye, quaintly, daintily, intellectually, glibly.' Emmeline Pethick-Lawrence was entranced by her. Christabel was no highbrow, she admitted, but 'her speeches were full of wit and a kind of challenge that suited her pretty youthful appearance ... It is no exaggeration to say that she taught the man in the street politics, as well as educating previously untrained women.' Even Sylvia, torn as so often between her admiration for her sister and her dislike of her politics, could not withhold her praise.

That she was slender, young, with the flawless colouring of the briar rose, and an easy grace cultivated by her enthusiastic practise of the dance [Christabel used to take time off for dancing lessons] were delicious embellishments to the sterner features of her discourse. Yet the real secret of her attraction was her audacity, fluent in its assurance, confidently gay.

But, added Sylvia grimly,

I detested her incipient Toryism; I was wounded by her frequent casting out of trusted friends for a mere hair's breadth difference of view; I often considered her policy mistaken, either in conception or in application; but her speaking delighted me.

With the resources of Clements Inn behind her, Christabel was able to notch up the campaign to a new intensity. The routine harrying of ministers was unpleasant enough for the participants. When, early in 1906, thirty women carrying banners marched on the residence of Asquith, then Chancellor of the Exchequer, the police fell on them, driving them off with fists and knees. Annie Kenney and two East End Suffragettes were sent to prison for six weeks for refusing to be bound over to keep the peace for a year. Emmeline Pankhurst herself was rough-handled for asking a question at one of Asquith's meetings. 'How would Mr Asquith have liked some of our experiences?' wrote Christabel.

Mice, poor little creatures, live and dead, flung at us, tomatoes, flour, stones, often concerted and continuous shouting and stamping. Sometimes at the open-air meetings we were in positive danger through the roughness of gangs of disturbers and the consequent surging of the crowds.

But worse was to come. Prison sentences were becoming routine. In fact, the Suffragettes positively invited them. Not for them the polite pestering of MPs which had been the hallmark of the constitutionalists. When they lobbied Parliament, demanding to see ministers, they refused to take 'No' for an answer and made a scene. Rough-handling and arrest followed automatically. One such scrimmage took place on 23 October 1906, on the reassembly of Parliament when WSPU women went into the lobby in relays and tried to make speeches there. Ten women were arrested when the police were called in to throw them out. On their appearance at Cannon Row Police Court the next day, Sylvia hurried round to intercede for them with the magistrate. She too was flung into the street and arrested as she tried to make a speech to the waiting crowd. She was charged with obstruction and abusive language, and sentenced to fourteen days in the Third Division, 'the worst the irritated magistrate could do for me'. She was now to have her first experience of the horrors of Holloway.

During the Suffragette struggle there were to be endless disputes with the authorities over the prison classification in which offenders should be placed. In the Third, or lowest Division, they were ranked as common criminals, wearing prison clothes, enduring the roughest conditions and eating prison food. In the Second Division conditions were only slightly better. The Suffragettes claimed passionately that they were political prisoners, not criminals, and should be placed as misdemeanants in the First Division, where they would have a wide range of privileges: the right to wear their own clothes, to see their friends and to have food, writing materials and other amenities brought in from outside. From the start the authorities were uncertain how to handle them. By tradition and by statute the English legal system had always ranked certain offences as political, but the definition of 'political' was neither comprehensive nor precise. Since the Home Secretary maintained that the classification was a matter for the courts, the Suffragettes were at the mercy of magistrates and judges who had little sympathy with their political arguments. The prison treatment of the Suffragettes was therefore to vary arbitrarily according to the mood of those who tried them or to the effectiveness of the political pressure on their behalf.

As Sylvia shared the prison conditions of common criminals – the filthy cells, coarse prison clothing, almost inedible food and dehumanizing treatment by the warders – it seemed to her obvious that the Suffragettes should make common cause with this other oppressed section of society and press for prison reform. Christabel thought otherwise. No distraction was to be allowed from her central aim. But Sylvia was not to be silenced. Thanks to protests in Parliament at the treatment of the Suffragettes, they were transferred to the First Division and she was able to send for her drawing materials. She comforted herself by sketching the squalor of the prison scenes and on her release gave interviews to the press on the need for prison reform, distributing her sketches as evidence.

Despite itself, the NUWSS was being driven into reluctant admiration for the Suffragettes. The idea that women could be sent to Holloway – and in the dreaded Third Division, too – shocked Millicent Fawcett and she publicly announced her support for the prisoners.

I hope the more old-fashioned suffragists will stand by them; and I take this opportunity of saying that in my opinion, far from having injured the movement, they have done more during the last twelve months to bring it within the region of practical politics than we have been able to accomplish in the same number of years.

The WSPU thanked Millicent Fawcett warmly for her support, and on the prisoners' release the NUWSS gave a banquet in their honour. For a time all was harmony.

But the attitude of the authorities was hardening and Christabel knew she must step up the pace. In February 1907 the triumvirate at Clements Inn decided to call a Women's Parliament to coincide with the opening of a new session of Parliament. It was to be the first of many to be held in the Caxton Hall, within easy reach of Westminster. Tickets were sold out days in advance and the Exeter Hall, which the NUWSS had barely filled a few days earlier, was hired for the overflow. The atmosphere was tense as the women sat waiting for news of the King's Speech. When word came that it contained no reference to women's suffrage, the meeting erupted. This was no time for futile resolutions. 'Rise up, women!' cried Emmeline Pankhurst and back came the answering shouts of 'Now!' Four hundred women streamed out of the hall to march to Westminster, led by Mrs Charlotte Despard, the wealthy philanthropist.

Sylvia's account of the event reads like a battle bulletin. The constables had been given orders to head the women off, making as few arrests as possible.

Mounted men scattered the marchers: foot police seized them by the back of the neck and rushed them along at arm's length, thumping them in the back, and bumping them with their knees in approved police fashion. Women, by the hundred, returned again and again with painful persistence, enduring this treatment by the hour. Those who took refuge in doorways were dragged down the steps and hurled in front of the horses, then pounced upon by constables and beaten again.

Even the usually hostile press was shocked. Next day the *Daily Chronicle* published a cartoon of a mounted policeman over the caption: 'The London Cossack'.

On one point Sylvia's account differed from Christabel's. It was not the last time their version of events was to diverge.

As I was leading out a little band, I was surprised to see Christabel slip quietly into the line behind me. She told me later that she thought it would be necessary for her to go to prison in London and on the spur of the moment she had decided to take this opportunity while sentences were short. She feared that if her absence were protracted, her influence might be undermined.

Christabel put a different gloss on her behaviour. 'These Women's Parliaments were an ordeal,' she recalled.

The tension, as the deputations went out to fight their way among the crowds and against the resistance of the police, was painful indeed. I was in the first advance of 1907. At other times I was on the platform to see others go and await the news – whether they were possibly admitted or probably repulsed – to receive them as they came back battered and bruised, to see them return to the struggle. This was almost worse than being with them in the fray. To be chairman or speaker at one of these Women's Parliaments was among the most testing experience of the movement.

She was increasingly to insist that it was her duty to keep

out of prison and out of the skirmishes, reserving herself for the task of leadership.

Despite the activities of the 'Cossacks' on that day, fifteen women managed to rush the police guard into the House and hold a meeting in the lobby. In all, fifty-four arrests were made, including Mrs Despard, Sylvia and Christabel. Prison sentences were handed out, ranging from seven days to three weeks, except for a workman, Edward Croft, who received one month for trying to protect a woman in Parliament Square.

This time prison was to be almost jolly. Thanks to the protective vigilance of supporters in Parliament, the women were placed in the First Division. It was bliss to be able to wear their own clothes, send for food from outside and have facilities for pursuing their professions or trades. The Suffragettes took full advantage of their privileges, tapping messages in Morse to each other on the hot-water pipes, shouting to other cells, talking in the exercise yard – even bursting into song. Sylvia continued her sketching of prison scenes. Christabel sent for her secretary. 'But,' she wrote later, 'even with First Division gilt on the bars, the fact of imprisonment is inimical to any initiative work. One could not have led from prison, as one could lead from exile,' an *ex post facto* justification of her own voluntary exile three years later.

Prison merely whetted the women's appetite for martyrdom, particularly as the legislative doors remained firmly closed to them. In March 1907 another Private Member's Bill on women's enfranchisement was talked out. In protest another Women's Parliament was organized in Caxton Hall, this time embellished by a crowd of cotton operatives in clogs and shawls, led by Annie Kenney. There was another march to Parliament Square where a thousand extra police had been drafted in. Seventy-five women were arrested and sent to prison. Sylvia noted that in 1906–7 Suffragettes served 191 weeks of prison sentences. In 1907–8 the figure rose to 350 weeks. Emmeline Pankhurst, who had been warned by the Registrar-General that she must curb her public activities, resigned her registrarship, giving up with barely a moment's hesitation her income, job and the pension that went with it. She was ready to give up life itself, she declared.

Clements Inn became a hive of activity. Weekly 'at homes' were started that became so popular they filled the Queen's Hall every Monday. Frederick Pethick-Lawrence gave up his *Labour Record* to launch the WSPU's own journal, *Votes for Women*, of which he and his wife were joint editors. Funds flowed in. Membership expanded. By August 1907 there were seventy branches up and down the country. 'How glorious those Suffragette days were!' reminisced Christabel. 'To lose the personal in the great impersonal is to live!'

No doubt none too happy in this self-congratulatory atmosphere, Sylvia decided to take a painting holiday. She wanted to study the conditions under which women worked in the black industrial belts. She started at Cradley Heath in Staffordshire's 'Black Country', painting the women making chains and nails. She was horrified at what she found: 'Never have I seen so hideous a disregard of elementary decencies in housing and sanitation as in that area.' She noted too that men earned good wages in the chain industry, while women earned a pittance working eight or ten hours a day at the domestic forge. She found the same harsh conditions and injustices in the shoe-making industry in Leicester and in the Lancashire cotton mills. She was happy again in being able to fuse her love of painting with her passion for politics, but she was called back sternly to Suffragette duty by her mother and Christabel from time to time, usually to help in by-elections; in these they vigorously pursued their policy of hounding the Liberal candidate, whatever his views on women's suffrage or anything else, because his own Liberal Government would not give women the vote. Inevitably, they found themselves helping the Tory candidate.

Sylvia found it increasingly irksome to have to suppress her socialist convictions for the women's cause. Her misery reached a new peak at the Bury St Edmunds by-election of 1907. It was another rural area, Sylvia tells us, 'where, in default of a Labour movement, such independence as was beginning to form among the workers regarded Liberalism as its only outlet from the dominant influence of the brewer, the parson and the squire'. The Tory candidate was a member of the great Guinness brewing family and Sylvia found it 'intensely saddening' to have to help strengthen the Tory bonds she longed to break. She also found herself in 'ill-assorted companionship' with ardent local Tory feminists. When the result was announced, she found she had helped to more than double the Tory majority. A great cheer went up in which she could not join. 'My gaze turned from the jubilant, well-dressed Tories on the balcony, across the laughing, non-Party masses of the crowd, to a little group of frowning workmen with red favours. My thoughts were sad.'

Back at Clements Inn she was interrogated as to why she had not joined in the cheers. She stood her ground and the subject was dropped. Thankfully, she escaped back to her painting tour. The gulf between her and Christabel was widening.

But for Sylvia blood was still thicker than politics. It was as though some umbilical cord that she could not break still tied her to her mother and sister. Discontent had been brewing in some quarters of the WSPU and she found herself in the ironical situation of being summoned home to help suppress a rebellion against Christabel's 'autocracy', the very autocracy of which she herself had complained. Expansion of WSPU membership had brought its dangers. Many of the newcomers to the ranks did not know the Pankhursts personally and among a number of those who did there was resentment at Christabel's calm assumption that the WSPU was the personal property of the triumvirate at Clements Inn. The leader of the dissidents was no less than Teresa Billington, one of the WSPU's most respected figures, who was now launching the alien idea that the control of the Union ought to be democratized. The previous year she had managed to force through the holding of an annual conference and the election of the central committee. Christabel had been deeply hurt. 'I was astonished at the suggestion,' she recalled, pointing out that

the WSPU had been founded and led by mother and myself, upon our own initiative and responsibility . . . We shaped the policy of the WSPU. We resolved upon and adopted militancy. Leaders, in fact, from the very beginning, though we ourselves did not intro-duce the title, we had continued to lead.

Christabel, in fact, was obsessed with leadership. She had acquiesced in the first election of the central committee grudgingly. It had gone her way and she had got the committee members she wanted, but as the second annual conference approached, she decided the time had come to assert herself. Things might not turn out so well this time.

'Certain unrest was felt, electioneering began, rumours ran concerning who would be re-elected and who would not.' Of course she and her mother and Emmeline Pethick-Lawrence were safe, but what if they did not get a committee which would do their will? 'Some, if not all, of our original choice and appointment might be replaced by others of a different point of view!' The idea was anathema. What if some of them had the same point of view as Sylvia? The election must be scotched. 'It was as though in the midst of a battle the Army began to vote upon who should command it, and what strategy should be.'

Sylvia, called in to help foil the machinations of Teresa Billington (now Mrs Billington-Greig), proved a broken reed. She could not see what all the fuss was about. 'You can carry the conference with you. There is no doubt of it,' she assured her mother. But Emmeline Pankhurst was taking no risks. She cancelled the conference and declared that henceforth she would appoint the central committee herself. So great was the magic of the Pankhurst name that she got away with it. The majority of the membership backed her and the dissidents had to break away and form their own Women's Freedom League.

Christabel dismissed the split as a matter of no consequence. 'There were now two militant organizations instead of one, and all ended happily ... Far from regretting the existence of a new militant society, we wished that all the other woman suffrage societies would turn militant.' Sylvia admitted that the Women's Freedom League never approached the WSPU in membership, means or influence, but she noted drily: 'The destruction of the democratic constitution prevented the WSPU from becoming a long-lived organization; the Freedom League remained when the WSPU was no more.'

The field was now clear for Christabel to declare total war against the Liberal Government. Discipline in the WSPU was tightened up. All members were called upon to sign a pledge: 'I endorse the objects and methods of the Women's Social and Political Union and hereby undertake not to support the candidate of any political party at Parliamentary elections until women have the vote.' Sylvia could not bring herself to sign it, although, still divided in her feelings, she continued to carry out the policy. 'The spirit of the WSPU now became more and more that of a volunteer army at war,' she noted.

Cabinet ministers, plagued by the persistent Suffragettes, no longer held open meetings. Admission was by ticket only. But they had underestimated their enemy. The forging of tickets was child's play for the WSPU. In desperation the organizers then excluded women from the meetings altogether. Thereupon the women went to extraordinary lengths to penetrate their guard, entering the meeting halls through windows and lying hidden for hours, springing out of their lairs to unfurl their banners and shout their slogans at the strategic moment. When they failed to get into a meeting, men sympathizers in the audience would take up the heckling on their behalf.

Nor were social occasions sacrosanct. Enormous trouble was taken at Clements Inn to track down ministers' social engagements and prepare an attack. Elegantly dressed women, looking the very pillars of the Establishment, would mingle with the guests at élite parties and suddenly accost ministers, raising their battle cry. It was all good fun, even when two Suffragettes, who had chained themselves to the railing of No. 10 Downing Street while the Cabinet was in session, were sent to prison for three weeks.

But the year 1908 was to produce new dangers for Christabel's strategy. The year opened badly enough. In January Asquith told a deputation of the non-militant NUWSS that the Government had no intention of giving women the vote. In the mid-Devon by-election campaign that same month Emmeline Pankhurst was lamed when she and a fellow Suffragette were mobbed by a rough gang, furious at the defeat of their Liberal candidate, which they blamed, with some justice, on the intervention of the Suffragettes. In the Leeds by-election campaign that followed she made a big impact by leading a torchlight procession of some 100,000 women to Hunslet Moor. When at the end of January the King's Speech at the opening of Parliament once again contained no mention of women's suffrage, another Women's Parliament at Caxton Hall decided to send another deputation to the Commons to deliver a resolution of protest to the Government. This time Christabel thought up the ingenious device of packing some of her dedicated supporters into a Trojan horse in the form of two furniture vans. When they successfully approached the entrance to the Commons, twenty-one women sprang out and made a dash for the doors. Two of them actually succeeded in getting in. Next morning forty-eight women received two months' imprisonment in the Second Division and two 'old offenders' got one month each in the dreaded Third Division. The privileges of the First Division were to be no more. It was war.

The Women's Parliament, still in session in Caxton Hall, reacted with typical defiance. Emmeline Pankhurst, back from Leeds and still limping from her mid-Devon injury, hauled herself on to the platform and announced that she would lead a deputation of thirteen women to Parliament in protest. Volunteers clamoured for the honour. The deputation set forth and Mrs Flora Drummond – known as the 'General' for her brisk efficiency – noticed Emmeline's limp and asked a passing stranger driving by in a dog cart if he would give Mrs Pankhurst a lift. He agreed and Emmeline climbed in. Christabel took up the tale in a note she wrote at the time:

Watching them in the street were many policemen and a curious crowd. There was something intensely moving in the sight of these women, one in a little humble cart, the others walking two by two behind. They were so small in strength, so few in number, and yet they had a purpose strong enough to overcome the resistance of the Government, supported as it is by every material resource. As the little procession moved away, a bystander said: 'That lot won't get far'; and so it was, for they had not gone many yards before the police fell upon them, ordered the leader out of the trap, and broke the ranks of those on foot.

Emmeline and her companions, having refused to be bound over, were sent to prison for six months in the Second Division.

But Easter 1908 was to bring a more serious blow. Campbell-Bannerman resigned and Asquith, hated enemy of the Suffragettes, succeeded him as Prime Minister. He had been dangerous enough as a member of the Cabinet. How much more dangerous he would be now he was in command! It was clear that he had, if anything, toughened his stand against the women. Rumour had it that his second wife, Margot Tennant, an ambitious socialite, detested the Suffragettes and was busy stiffening his hostility. Be that as it may, it was clear he had no intention of giving in to them. Yet, as a result of the rough-handling of the Suffragettes, public sympathy for them was beginning to grow. He had to find ways of deflecting that sympathy. It became a battle of wits between him and Christabel.

Christabel had one asset on her side. Liberal women, disturbed by their Government's brutal suppression of the women's agitation, were beginning to rebel. The annual conference of the Women's Liberal Federation was about to be held and resolutions were sent in demanding that Liberal women should refuse to work in elections unless women's suffrage was granted before the dissolution of the Parliament. The situation was made worse when a Liberal MP, H. Y. Stanger, was successful in the Private Members' ballot and introduced a Women's Enfranchisement Bill. The Bill even got a Second Reading by 271 votes to 92, but the Speaker ruled that instead of going into committee upstairs, all its stages must be taken on the floor of the House, which meant it would be crowded out by other business unless the Government allotted it part of its own time. On the eve of the conference sixty Liberal MPs went on a deputation to Asquith, urging him to give the Bill the necessary time.

Asquith was ready for them. He saw the opportunity of killing two birds with one stone. The widening of the franchise, for men at any rate, had long been an important part of Liberal policy. He could use this to divert the discontent. He therefore told the deputation that he regretted he could not facilitate the passage of the Stanger Bill, which he hinted was a puny measure anyway. The Government had its eye on bigger things.

Franchise reform had always been a plank of Liberal policy, he told them, and, 'barring accidents', he regarded it as a 'binding obligation' for his Government to introduce a far-reaching Reform Bill before the Parliament came to an end. The Reform Bill would not include women, but he assured them that an opportunity would be given for a women's suffrage amendment to be moved and, as long as it was framed on democratic lines, the Government would leave the decision to a free vote of the House.

The ploy worked. Presiding over the Liberal conference the next morning, Lady Carlisle declared: 'Our great Prime Minister, all honour to him, has opened a way to us, by which we can enter into that inheritance from which we have been too long debarred.' Sylvia remarked acidly, 'The loyalty of the women Liberals was assured for another year at least.'

While the constitutional suffragists hesitated, Christabel denounced the whole thing as a trick. The women, she exclaimed, would not be fooled. In a letter to *The Times* she accused Asquith of the 'old Liberal policy of delay, the fruits of which we have seen so often before'. Her scepticism was vindicated when a Liberal MP asked Asquith in the House what would happen if a women's amendment to the proposed Reform Bill were carried. 'My honourable friend has asked me a contingent question with regard to a remote and speculative future,' replied the Prime Minister loftily. Triumphant Suffragettes said, 'We told you so!' He was obviously dodging. Christabel was right when she argued that only direct action would move the Government.

Their response was to organize a series of provincial demonstrations, culminating in a massive rally in Hyde Park on Midsummer Day 1908. It was another brilliant feat of organization. Emmeline Pethick-Lawrence suggested that the WSPU should have its own colours. Purple, white and green were chosen and emblazoned on the hundreds of banners, thousands of flags, ribbons and regalia, with borders and heraldic devices, which Sylvia designed. Special trains were run from seventy towns. Twenty platforms were set up for the speakers and a quarter of a million handbills distributed. Decorated buses drove through the streets and a steam launch laden with Suffragettes stopped opposite the House of Commons to taunt the MPs taking tea on the terrace. Frederick Pethick-Lawrence, directing proceedings from a conning tower erected in the middle of the Hyde Park mêlée, reported that 'the numbers who came to the park that day were greater than had ever been gathered together before on any one spot in the history of the world'. *The Times* hazarded the guess that there could have been a quarter of a million people there, or perhaps more. A resolution demanding votes for women was dispatched to Asquith by special messenger. He replied curtly that he had nothing to add to the statement he had already made.

It was clear that rallies, however spectacular, were not enough. There must be another march on Parliament, when the House reassembled. This time it must put all their other marches in the shade. A preparatory demonstration to rally support was held in Trafalgar Square and a leaflet that was to give the Government its chance was distributed. It read: 'Men and Women – Help the Suffragettes to Rush the House of Commons'. According to Christabel, there had been long discussion about which word to use. 'Raid', 'invade', 'besiege' and 'storm' had all been rejected as not quite right. Someone suggested 'rush' and 'rush' it was. It was to prove extremely provocative to the authorities.

Christabel, Emmeline Pankhurst and Flora Drummond

proclaimed the message from the plinth in Trafalgar Square. Unknown to them at the time, Lloyd George, now Chancellor of the Exchequer, was listening in the crowd. A few days later the three women were summoned to appear at Bow Street, charged with 'inciting the public to a certain wrongful and illegal act, viz. to rush the House of Commons at 7.30 p.m. on October 13th inst.'. They bided their time for twenty-four hours, then gave themselves up at the very moment the march was planned to start. A mass of infuriated women took their place in it.

The 'conspiracy' trial of the three women, which opened at Bow Street the next day, was to be the peak point of Christabel's fame and popularity. Summoning up her legal skills, she decided to conduct their defence herself. Her demand for trial by jury was rejected by the magistrate, but she managed to call Lloyd George and Herbert Gladstone, the Home Secretary, as witnesses. The idea of a young woman cross-examining Cabinet Ministers caught the public's imagination and Christabel took full advantage of her opportunity. 'For two days the Court was turned into a Suffragette meeting by a crowd of witnesses,' wrote Sylvia. Christabel's fans multiplied. Max Beerbohm wrote in the *Saturday Review*:

She has all the qualities which an actress needs and of which so few actresses have any . . . Her whole being is alive with her every meaning, and if you can imagine a very graceful rhythmic dance done by a dancer who uses not her feet, you will have some idea of Miss Pankhurst's method.

Sylvia, describing the scene three years later in her book *The Suffragette*, published in New York, outdid Max Beerbohm in hyperbole. Whether her childhood love for her sister had rekindled, or whether she had hyped up her prose for an American readership, it is difficult to say.

In her fresh white muslin dress whose one note of color was the broad band of purple, white and green stripes around her waist, with her soft brown hair uncovered, the little silky curls with just a hint of gold in them clustering around her neck, and in this dingy place her skin looking even more brilliantly white and those rose-petal cheeks of hers even more exquisitely and vividly flushed with purest pink than usual, she was as bright and dainty as a newly opened flower, and with all her look of perfect health and vigor, appeared so slender and so delicately knit as to have little more of substance in her than a briar rose.

The contrast between Christabel and Lloyd George ('the contrast between the buoyancy of the girl and the depression of the statesman', as Max Beerbohm put it) was not to the magistrate's liking. After two days of this he had had enough and closed the case. He sentenced Emmeline Pankhurst and Flora Drummond to three months in the Second Division and Christabel to ten weeks. But Christabel had made her mark. The *Daily News* commented that her 'subtlety and audacity' as a counsel should break down the ban on women barristers.

While Christabel fretted in prison, which she hated, Sylvia was in charge at Clements Inn. It was her turn to sit in the office and send the women into battle. She proved as in-genious as Christabel in insinuating them into the front row of a mass meeting at the Albert Hall which Lloyd George was to address, arranging for them to wear facsimile prison dress under their cloaks and to throw off the cloaks when the time came to interrupt. In the deserted office she waited impatiently for the women to return. 'They came in ones and twos, bruised and dishevelled, hatless, with hair dragged down and clothing torn; some had their very corsets ripped off, false teeth knocked out, faces scratched, eyes swollen, noses bleeding.' The stewards had excelled themselves in violence. As the news leaked out of the treatment of the women, public opinion began to be uneasy. Even the fact that one Suffragette, Helen Ogston, had laid about her with a dog whip, complaining that a man had put the lighted end of his cigar on her wrist while others had struck her in the chest, did not alienate the reporters' sympathy. After all, who could blame the women for defending themselves? The *Manchester Guardian* reflected the views of more than one newspaper when it wrote that the women had been ejected 'with a brutality that was almost nauseating'.

Yet the Government remained obdurate. Patronizing amusement at the antics of the Suffragettes gave way to exasperation. It would show them! Attempts were made to tighten up the law. When Muriel Matters of the Women's Freedom League leapt up in the Ladies' gallery in the House of Commons and harangued the startled MPs, it was found she could not be ejected because she had chained herself to the gallery grille behind which the women were delicately immured. The Government therefore tried to hurry through the 'Brawling Bill' to make disturbances in the House a punishable offence. This was laughed out of court and the Government responded by closing the gallery to any woman not sponsored by an MP as a relative. The baiting of Lloyd George at the Albert Hall produced another Bill providing for a fine of £5 (a big sum in those days) or a month's imprisonment for 'disorderly conduct' at a public meeting, though, in fact, it remained practically a dead letter.

Magistrates dealt with the Suffragettes more severely. Prison conditions became harsher. Leniency was out.

In this impasse there was one serious flaw in Christabel's strategy. Asquith had a trump card she could not play. She had a few thousand dedicated members. He had the loyalty of a mass party which would not desert him when the chips were down. Liberals and Labour M Ps alike were more concerned with the condition of the people than with the grievances of a million comfortably-off women. To them the social condition of Britain, with its unemployment, searing poverty, sweated labour and slums, was so appalling that social reform must be given priority. And for all his limitations Asquith was head of a great reforming Government which was about to embark on an historic showdown with the House of Lords, the refuge of hereditary privilege.

Against this Christabel could set only the heroism of a few determined women. She could win an argument but not a vote. Although Liberal M Ps helped to carry the Second Reading of Stanger's Bill by 271 votes to 91, few of them were prepared to defy to the end a government that was struggling to defend its reforming programme against the House of Lords. Their Lordships had grudgingly let through an Old Age Pensions Bill, giving a pension of 5s a week for those with an income of less than 8s a week (though Lord Rosebery muttered that 'a scheme so prodigal of expenditure' could deal 'a blow at the Empire which could be almost mortal'). But they were digging their heels in over the Government's attempt to introduce universal free education and were shaping up to reject Lloyd George's 'People's Budget', which was on its way. This was no time to rock the boat.

Labour M Ps went even further in their distrust of the

Suffragettes, or at least of Christabel's policies. Her demand for the 'Limited Vote This Session', her indifference to wider reform, exasperated them. Why enfranchise one million propertied women 'immediately', as she was demanding, when they would only add to the Tory vote? The social condition of the country would be improved only when working men and women had the vote, so adult suffrage was the only answer. But Christabel was actively resisting this. She had deliberately narrowed her vision down to the single issue of equality with men in whatever inadequate franchise might be available.

Indeed, she had got herself into the anomalous position of actively opposing the widening of the vote. The more limited the franchise, she argued, the more likely were women to be included in it. When a well-meaning MP, Geoffrey Howard, won a place in the Private Members' ballot and devoted it to a Bill to give manhood and womanhood suffrage on a three months' residential qualification, which would have increased the electorate to 30 million, she promptly denounced the unhappy man as a traitor. He had, she declared, drawn a red herring across the path by bringing in an omnibus measure 'in which the issue of women's enfranchisement was entangled with, and indeed strangled by, proposals for revolutionizing the franchise as a whole'. Unfortunately, the other suffrage societies took the same line so, although the Second Reading of this far-reaching measure was carried by 35 votes, Asquith was able to brush it aside. Sylvia was bitterly disappointed.

If only the women's suffrage movement had had any vision, she argued, it would have seized on the Bill as a chance to get women the vote as part of a comprehensive move to adult suffrage. But, she added sadly, 'the time for this was not yet'.

Christabel's tunnel vision increasingly worried her. She was afraid that the women's suffrage movement was turning in on itself and that its activities would begin to stale. And, indeed, as 1909 progressed, and the familiar forms of protest were rolled out, that danger seemed imminent. Although mass gatherings were organized, more and more women arrested, by-election candidates pestered and ingenious means found of circumventing the 'no women admitted' rule which was now in force at all Cabinet Ministers' meetings (at one Free Trade Hall meeting a Suffragette hid in the box all through the previous night), there were signs that the novelty was beginning to wear off, despite some aristocratic embellishments, as when the ethereal, but ardent, Lady Constance Lytton insisted on going to prison with the rest. But it was all getting a bit repetitive.

To enliven the Suffragettes' image, Sylvia was set to work producing a motif for the WSPU. This depicted an angel in flowing robe, blowing a trumpet and carrying a standard bearing the word 'Freedom'. It appeared everywhere: on WSPU banners, its programmes and even on a Suffragette tea service. She designed a WSPU greeting card showing a maiden sowing seeds and carrying a quotation from James Russell Lowell: 'What men call luck is the prerogative of valiant souls, the fealty life pays its rightful kings'. Suffragettes who had been to prison were presented with a 'Holloway brooch' which Sylvia had designed, depicting a portcullis emblazoned with a broad arrow in the Suffragette colours, with silver chains hanging on either side. With it they were given an illuminated address signed by Emmeline

Pankhurst, also Sylvia's work. It all helped to maintain morale.

But the WSPU's most colourful venture was a mammoth exhibition in the Prince's Skating Rink, Knightsbridge. It was a remarkable feat of Clements Inn organization, but the artistic credit was Sylvia's. She was given three months to transform the large, stark hall into an appropriate setting for a festival and she succeeded triumphantly. With the help of half a dozen art students she decided to clothe the lofty walls with canvas panels twenty feet high decorated with symbolic designs and encased in pilasters and round arches of interlacing vines. The canvases were so huge that she had to search London for a room big enough for her and her helpers to work on them, but, though the work was laborious, her spirits soared as she let her creative fancy run through a William Morris world of flowering almond trees, springing flowers and elaborate tracery, with the green

WSPU design embossed on the cover of bound copies of *Votes for Women*, 1908

Design of the Holloway brooch

of the vines and purple of the grapes against the creamy white walls picking out the Suffragette colours delicately.

She chose the motif too, combining the pelican, symbol of sacrifice, with the dove of hope carrying the olive branch of peace and the broad arrow, badge of imprisonment, gilded and draped with the laurels of victory. Throughout the whole hall ran the theme: 'He that goeth forth and weepeth bearing precious seed shall doubtless come again rejoicing, bringing his sheaves with him'. The effect was completed by the towering figures of two women thirteen feet high painted at each end of the hall. At one end the woman was scattering the grain; at the other she was carrying the corn. The Suffragettes certainly knew how to put themselves across.

When the work was finished and the visitors came crowding in, Sylvia was exhilarated, even though she had

79

worked through the last two nights to finish it on time. Her ability to work all night was to become legendary. For all her nervous depressions Sylvia had stamina.

Frederick Pethick-Lawrence told an amusing anecdote about this brilliantly successful fair. Two girls asked him to introduce them to Emmeline Pankhurst and, when he did so, asked her shyly whether they might make an odd request. Could they look at her feet? 'My feet?' replied an astonished Mrs Pankhurst, lifting her long skirt. 'There,' said one girl to the other, 'our shop-mates were all wrong when they said the Suffragettes had large feet. Hers are unusually small!'

Her spirit refreshed by creative activity, Sylvia allowed herself the indulgence of a short painting holiday in a cottage on Cinder Hill near Penshurst. But the respite was brief. She was called back by the illness of her beloved younger brother, Harry, and when he died of infantile paralysis her mother, whom Sylvia accused in her heart of thoughtlessly neglecting him, 'was broken as I have never seen her; huddled together without a care for her appearance, she seemed an old, plain, cheerless woman. Her utter dejection moved me more than her vanished charm.' The family ties of the Pankhursts, despite their disagreements, were hard to break.

Sylvia also returned to an ugly development in the WSPU's battle with the Government. Some of its livelier members, frustrated by the Government's refusal to move an inch and tired of being always on the receiving end of injury, took matters into their own hands and resorted to stone-throwing, hurling stones wrapped in WSPU propaganda through the windows of government buildings. When arrested, they claimed the right of political status and, when it was refused, went on hunger strikes. After a few days, when they were weak with fasting, a bewildered Government ordered their release.

Dr Richard Pankhurst, beloved
husband and father, c. 1896

Emmeline Pankhurst as
honorary secretary of the
Women's Social and Political
Union she founded in 1903

The little girls of Russell
Square: Sylvia eight, Adela five
and Christabel ten, c. 1892

In Trafalgar Square Christabel incites women to 'rush the House of Commons', 11 October 1908

In the dock at Bow Street: Christabel with 'General' Flora Drummond and mother Emmeline, October 1908

Suffragettes campaign against the Liberals in the general election of 1910

Sylvia's charcoal, chalk and crayon portrait of Keir Hardie, c. 1910

Christabel and Sylvia

The Women's Coronation
Procession, 1911

Sylvia's decorations from the Prince's Skating Rink Exhibition
enliven another Suffragette bazaar at the Portman Rooms,
December 1911

Sylvia making converts at her new Suffragette headquarters in the
East End, 1912

At Trouville Annie Kenney and Emmeline Pankhurst recuperate
with Christabel from their prison ordeal, 1913

Police remove Emmeline
Pankhurst from the gates of
Buckingham Palace as she
tries to lead a deputation to
the King, May 1914

Helped by waiting friends, Sylvia leaves Holloway Prison, May 1921

Sylvia relaxes with her son, Richard, at Red Cottage, 1930

Sylvia leads a protest to the House of Commons against a proposal
to return Eritrea and Somaliland to the Italians, April 1948

At first the new tactic seemed highly effective. Stone-throwing meant a quick arrest without the misery of being knocked about; hunger striking meant earlier release. But Asquith, now at the flood tide of his constitutional battle with the Lords, was in no mood to be made a fool of by a few wild women. He would be a match for them. Sylvia could see what was coming. 'I believed then and always,' she explained, 'that the movement required, not more serious militancy by a few, but a stronger appeal to the great masses to join the struggle.' Despite this she could not bring herself to expostulate. 'I would rather have died at the stake than say one word against the actions of those who were in the throes of the fight.' But she added: 'I knew only too surely that the militant women would be made to suffer renewed hardships for each act of more serious damage.'

And so it proved. In September 1909 ten women, thwarted in their attempts to get into a meeting addressed by the Prime Minister in Birmingham, took their revenge. Two of them climbed on to the roof with axes in their hands, hacked off slates and threw them on to the roof of the hall. They were brought down when firemen were called to drench them with a hose. Eight others were arrested for window breaking, one of them for hurling an iron bar through the window of an empty carriage in the train carrying the Prime Minister back to London. They received sentences ranging from four months down to fourteen days and promptly went on hunger strike. Egged on by the public outcry at the women's damage to property, the Home Secretary ordered that they were to be forcibly fed by a rubber tube passed through the mouth or nose. A new horror now faced the Suffragettes.

The bravery of the women under this barbaric ordeal was to win them a permanent place among the heroines of history. They not only suffered intense pain, but they risked serious injury. One medical expert, consulted by the WSPU, testified that the results of persistent forcible feeding would be 'seriously to injure the constitution, to lacerate the parts surrounding the mouth, to break and ruin the teeth . . . to injure the digestive organs, to aggravate any bronchial condition which may exist and to cause dangerous chronic symptoms'. Keir Hardie and others protested in the House of Commons. Liberal journalists like H. N. Brailsford and H. W. Nevinson expressed their disgust. Dr Forbes Ross of Harley Street wrote in the *Observer*: 'As a medical man without any particular feeling for the cause of the Suffragettes, I consider forcible feeding by the methods employed an act of brutality beyond common endurance.' But the protests were ridiculed in the House of Commons, the Home Secretary having assured MPs that forcible feeding was 'hospital treatment', intended to save the women from themselves.

Christabel, too, was worried by the turn of events. She could see that more violent acts by the women would bring only greater brutality down on their heads. She was not, therefore, sorry when at the end of 1909 Asquith decided to go to the country to get support for his battle with the House of Lords. She thankfully declared that militancy would be suspended for the duration of the election, but that did not mean she had an iota of sympathy for the Government's policies. She was indifferent to the fact that a great constitutional struggle was going on, the Lords having thrown out Lloyd George's budget, thus violating the deeply rooted convention that control over taxation was the pre-rogative of the elected House.

Once again, under Christabel's leadership, the Suffragettes appeared unmoved by the political turmoil around them and the social unrest with which Lloyd George's budget was designed to deal. Here was a revolutionary measure that set out to switch resources from rich to poor through increased income tax and death duties, a Super Tax on high incomes to help pay for the old-age pensions the Government had introduced, the payment of family allowances and – greatest crime of all in the eyes of the landed aristocracy – the levying of a tax on the development value of land from which fortunes were being made. 'This is a War Budget,' Lloyd George told the House of Commons. 'It is for raising money to wage implacable warfare against poverty and squalidness.' But this had not prevented the Suffragettes from trying to wreck the Limehouse meeting at which he was seeking to mobilize public support for his Bill, then fighting its way through the House of Commons. Even Sylvia seemed strangely unstirred. 'Though the Lloyd George budget of 1909, with its taxation of land values and licensing duties, was widely advertised as a "War Budget Against Poverty",' she wrote, 'little enthusiasm for it could be worked up.'

The Suffragettes also seemed indifferent to the growing threat of war and the ominous naval arms race with Germany. The revolutionary new battleship, *Dreadnought*, appeared on the scene and the Tory Opposition in the Commons clamoured: 'We want eight and we won't wait.' Jingoist fever was rising. A handful of Liberals, Keir Hardie and a group of Labour pacifists were almost alone as they struggled against the tide.

During the election campaign of January 1910, Asquith renewed his pledge that, in the event of his Government introducing its promised Reform Bill, the inclusion of an amendment giving votes to women would be left to a free vote of the House. Christabel, ever optimistic, proclaimed that victory was near. She failed to read the message of the election result. Asquith, having called an election to strengthen his hand against the Lords, lost one hundred seats and was left with a majority of only two over the Conservatives. He was therefore dependent on the votes of eighty-two Irish Nationalists and forty Labour MPs in his battle with the Conservatives now breathing down his neck. Most of the Labour Members were sympathetic to the women's cause, but did not want to jeopardize the success of Asquith's battle with the Lords. The Irish Nationalists had their own sectarian row to hoe. They wanted to keep a Liberal Government in power at any cost until they got Home Rule. The outlook was hardly propitious for Christabel. There was barely a murmur of protest from MPs when the King's Speech was found to consist of only one legislative measure: the restriction of the veto power of the Lords. Liberal suffragist MPs obliged their Government by not balloting for a women's suffrage Bill in the Private Members' ballot. Women's suffrage seemed to have been submerged again.

Undismayed, Christabel renewed the truce. She and the Pethick-Lawrences had been in secret conclave with H. N. Brailsford, who was bringing together MPs of all parties in a Conciliation Committee, under the chairmanship of Lord Lytton, to draw up an agreed suffrage compromise. Moreover, King Edward VII died and political controversy was muted for the funeral. 'Votes for Women', black-bordered, carried the portrait of Queen Alexandra on its cover and the following week that of her successor, Queen Mary. Sylvia noted sarcastically: 'Christabel, daughter of the Republican Dr Pankhurst, vied with the Conservative organs in her expressions of devotion to the throne.' It was the shape of things to come.

In June 1910 the Conciliation Committee produced its

compromise: a Bill to give votes for women householders and women occupiers of business premises with a rateable value of not less than £10 per year. Sylvia was appalled. It would enfranchise merely one million women, mainly elderly women and spinsters. Though not expressly excluding married women, it provided that husband and wife could not get a vote for the same property. Yet under the existing law two men could qualify as joint householders or occupiers of the same property. So women were excluded who would not have been excluded if they were men. Such unequal treatment, she believed, could create a dangerous precedent for a suffrage reform Bill.

Christabel, however, jumped at it. 'My strongest, but unspoken reason for welcoming the Conciliation movement,' she confessed in her autobiography, 'was that it might avert the need for stronger militancy and would at least postpone the use thereof. Mild militancy was more or less played out.' She knew that 'milder acts' were becoming monotonous and that a pause would give time for familiarity to fade, so that they could be used again with fresh effect. She knew too that some of her devoted followers were in revolt against the one-sided violence being used against them by the Government and wanted to respond with greater violence. She could not hold them in much longer.

The vast majority of women's organizations endorsed the Bill. Public opinion and most of the press welcomed it. A few days later it was introduced to the House amid acclaim. But Asquith was in no hurry to move. He too could play the 'single issue' card and he was totally obsessed with his manœuvres over the House of Lords. Ireland was drifting towards civil war and Britain was swept with a wave of industrial unrest that made the granting of the vote to one million women seem insignificant. When he at last agreed to a Second Reading, which was carried by 299 votes to 189, the signs were still not encouraging. Asquith, Churchill and Lloyd George voted against the Bill, the latter arguing that it was too limited. The Bill was sent to a committee of the whole House as before, which meant it could only proceed with Government backing. The prospects had not changed at all.

Time was on Asquith's side. The House went into summer recess and when it was recalled in November he announced that a conference on Lords' reform had broken down and that he was going to the country again. There would be no time for the Conciliation Bill.

The truce was at an end. A few days later another Women's Parliament sent a deputation of three hundred women to Westminster. They were treated, wrote Sylvia, with 'unexampled violence'. For six hours the women were battered. Sylvia and Annie Kenney, under instructions to avoid arrest this time, drove to the scene in a taxi to record what was going on.

Finding it unbearable thus to watch other women knocked about, with a violence more than common even on such occasions, we jumped out of the taxi, but soon returned to it for policemen in uniform and plain clothes struck us in the chest, seized us by the arms and flung us to the ground. This was a common experience. . . Two girls with linked arms were being dragged about by two uniformed policemen. One of a group of officers in plain clothes ran up and kicked one of the girls, whilst the others laughed and jeered at her.

The eighteenth of November 1910 was to be known as Black Friday in the annals of the Suffragettes.

The movement had begun to claim its dead.

I saw Cecilia Haig go out with the rest [wrote Sylvia], a tall, strongly built, reserved woman, comfortably situated, who in ordinary circumstances might have gone through life without ever receiving an insult, much less a blow. She was assaulted with violence and indecency and died in December, 1911, after a painful illness, arising from her injuries. Henria Williams, already suffering from a weak heart, did not recover from the treatment she received that night in the Square, and died on January 1st.

Just before Christmas 1910 Emmeline Pankhurst's sister, Mary Clarke, newly released from prison, died from a stroke, 'too frail to weather this rude tide of militant struggle'.

The treatment of the militants was now shot through with sexual undertones. At moments it seemed as if the women would be faced not merely with violence but with rape. 'Be careful! They are dragging women down the side streets!' went up the frightened cry. On the Government's side all pretence of chivalry was abandoned. On her side Christabel was developing an almost mystical sense of women's vocation as the purifiers of the race. It was no longer a question of women liberating women, but of women liberating society as a whole from men's carnality. Emmeline Pethick-Lawrence was very much in tune with this mystical sense of destiny. As she put it in 'The Undercurrent of the Woman's Movement', an article she had written for *Votes for Women* a few months earlier, 'there are times when we are conscious that underneath this political struggle there is a great moral and spiritual Movement, controlled not by ourselves, but by those forces we call the forces of evolution'. The aim was not only to win the freedom of women's body and mind. 'The Woman's Movement is working out the freedom of the woman's soul, whose emergence into the world of action is the new hope of the future.'

One hundred and fifteen women and two men were arrested on Black Friday, but when they appeared at Bow Street most of the charges were withdrawn. With a general election in the offing, the Government wanted to appear conciliatory. Only those accused of window breaking or assaults on the police were proceeded against. Five days later, on the eve of dissolution, Asquith made his promised statement to the House on women's suffrage: 'The government will, if they are still in power, give facilities in the next Parliament for effectively proceeding with a Bill, if so framed as to admit of free amendment.' Not surprisingly, the women greeted the statement with derision. The loopholes were obvious. What sort of a Bill would it be, and when? Emmeline Pankhurst immediately led a march to No. 10. The police hastily formed a cordon and the 'Battle of Downing Street' ensued. 'Mrs Pankhurst was in the middle of the struggle and all its danger,' wrote Christabel.

She had a marvellous way of remaining, in the midst of the crowds and struggles, as calm and proudly dignified as a queen going to her coronation – or perhaps to the scaffold in some un-righteous rebellion against her proper majesty.

It was the last militancy before the second election of 1910. Taking advantage of the lull, Sylvia went on a lecture tour of America, where her mother had had a triumphal reception a year earlier. Like her mother, she did an extensive tour: 'East through Canada to St John's, New Brunswick, West to California, South to Tennessee', carrying the Suffragette message to crowded halls and enthusiastic audiences. With her she took her book, *The Suffragette*, which was to be published in New York. 'I had arrived at the height of the interest and sympathy felt in America in the English movement,' she records in her autobiography. In Iowa, where a Bill to give Iowa women the vote was pending, she was even asked to address a joint convention of the Senate and the House of Representatives. Typically, she insisted everywhere on visiting prisons, factories, laundries, and was shocked at the conditions she often found. Nonetheless, the youthful vigour of American life attracted her and she toyed with the idea that 'some day I might become an American citizen'.

Sylvia returned early in 1911 to find the election had left the Parliamentary situation at home practically unchanged, with Liberals and Conservatives neck and neck and the Government once again dependent on Irish Nationalist and Labour Party votes. No less than three MPs who had been successful in the Private Members' ballot were ready to introduce the Conciliation Bill, suitably modified. Sylvia noted scornfully: 'The Bill now applies only to women house-holders. The £10 occupiers (usually poor lodgers in un-furnished rooms) were thrown out as a sop to Liberal democratic ideas.' Nonetheless, the suffrage societies welcomed it avidly and when in May 1911 the Second Reading was carried by the massive majority of 255 votes to 88, they concentrated all their efforts on pressurizing the Government to give it facilities. 'Never has such continuous and truly national support, representative of all classes and parties, been behind any measure brought before Parliament,' wrote Christabel. 'What a graceful thing it would be to gladden women and set them politically free in Coronation Year!'

But once again hopes were to be dashed. Two weeks later

Lloyd George announced that the Government stood by its promise to give the Bill facilities, but not in this session. It was prepared in the next session, if the Bill was again read a second time, to allot it a week for its further stages. The delay was ominous. And why just a week of Parliamentary time? What if the Bill's opponents filibustered again and used up the week?

At Clements Inn the organizers agonized. That summer the new King, George V, was to be crowned. Militancy or no militancy at coronation time? Reassuring noises came from the Government through Sir Edward Grey. The Government's offer was not bogus. Obstructors would not be allowed to wreck the Bill. If at the end of the promised week Parliament voted to carry on, the Government would not intervene. It sounded fair enough and Sir Edward was an honest man. Thankfully Christabel was able to indulge her 'national feeling and loyalty'. She admitted: 'We were glad to be able to justify to ourselves a non-militant policy.'

Together with all the other suffrage bodies, the WSPU now organized a great patriotic display, 'The Women's Coronation Procession'. Even Sylvia joined in enthusiastically. 'Upwards of forty thousand marched five abreast, taking three hours to pass a given point,' she rejoiced. 'It was a triumph of organization, a pageant of science, art, nursing, education, poverty, factorydom, slumdom, youth, age, labour, motherhood: a beautiful and imposing spectacle.' But she remained uneasy, convinced that the suffrage battle was not yet won.

And she was angry too when the women's suffrage movement opposed the National Insurance Bill, which introduced sickness and unemployment benefit, on the grounds that women had had no part in framing it. How could they be so indifferent to social reform? 'I could not content myself with destructive criticism of this far-reaching legislation,' she protested, 'but worked in conjunction with Keir Hardie preparing amendments to increase the proposed benefits.'

Her fears for the future were soon justified. In July 1911 the battle with the Lords was effectively ended when Asquith announced that the King had consented to create enough new peers to swamp the continuing opposition in the Lords to the Government's legislation. After great heart-searching, the Lords climbed down and accepted a curtailment of their powers instead, though by a small majority. The victory was to have a profound effect on the fortunes of the Suffragettes. In the first place the removal of the Lords' veto opened the way to Home Rule for Ireland, with which so many Liberals sympathized. The Irish Nationalists were determined to seize their advantage and to keep the Liberal Government in office 'at any cost'. Any sympathy they may have had with the wrecking tactics of the Suffragettes evaporated, not least because of the rumour that Asquith would resign if women's suffrage were to be carried against his will. Asquith was assured of a majority for his tough line.

A second consequence of Lords' reform was, in Christabel's eyes, equally dangerous. The way was now clear for the widening of the franchise for men which the Government had promised three years earlier. In November 1911 Asquith assured a deputation from the People's Suffrage Federation, led by the Labour spokesman Arthur Henderson, that the Government would introduce a Franchise Reform Bill the following year. He personally was against including women, but the House of Commons would be free to choose. Christabel promptly declared: 'War is declared on women!' It was a trick to scupper the Conciliation Bill. A united horde of suffrage societies descended on the Prime Minister and Christabel was not assuaged when he assured them that, if the Commons carried a women's suffrage amendment, the Government would accept that it was an integral part of the Bill and give it full facilities. She did not trust him an inch.

Lloyd George seemed to vindicate her suspicions when he declared at a meeting that the Conciliation Bill had been 'torpedoed'. This, he argued, left the road clear for including the working man's wife in the Franchise Reform Bill. Retorted Christabel: 'We only wished that it had! ... Our joy would have been boundless had we believed that the next year would see these millions of women enfranchised. But we knew that this would not happen.' Even Sylvia placed no faith in Lloyd George's words, though it was rumoured he supported women's suffrage in Cabinet. Did he, radical minister as he was, really believe in votes for women or was he merely making gestures of support, secure in the knowledge that he was in a minority in Cabinet? Certainly Lloyd George was not prepared to sacrifice the Liberal Party to the women's cause. He was not prepared to support a Conciliation Bill that would enfranchise only Tory women. All women must be enfranchised, or none at all.

The non-militants of the NUWSS were more optimistic about the Government's intentions than were the Suffragettes. Beavering away at their intimate discussions with political leaders and MPs, they were convinced that they could win support for women's amendments to the Franchise Reform Bill, while keeping the Conciliation Bill position as a fall-back. So they wanted to trust Lloyd George and, above all, they dreaded a return to militancy, which they believed would shatter the support they had carefully garnered. Christabel dismissed their views contemptuously.

She would never trust, or support, the machinations of Liberal ministers.

So the call to militancy went out again. The WSPU rank and file responded enthusiastically. Money poured into the WSPU to fuel the fight. Collections at the big rallies sometimes reached £10,000. Tired of the physical battering they got on deputations, Suffragettes now resorted to an orgy of window breaking as a way of getting arrested without injury. According to Sylvia, it was skilfully organized.

Motors were driven at dusk to quiet country lanes where flints could be obtained. Would-be window breakers met Marion Wallace Dunlop, or some other trusted member of the WSPU, at somebody's flat, and were furnished with hammers or black bags filled with flints.

They then made their way by taxi to where they would jump out and throw their stones. Some were arrested, but others succeeded in making a quick get-away. Government buildings were attacked and the windows of the National Liberal Club broken.

Other, more violent activities began to creep in – as yet unauthorized by Clements Inn. Emily Wilding Davison was arrested as she thrust a lighted, paraffin-saturated rag into a pillar box. A young member of the Men's Political Union flung his dispatch case through the window of Lloyd George's car, bruising the Chancellor's cheek. It was soon to be no holds barred. 'The year that opened in sunshine ended in storm,' wrote Christabel. The NUWSS issued a manifesto denouncing the militants.

Unfortunately for the Suffragettes there were far more serious storms to distract the Government and the country as 1912 dawned. Winston Churchill was sent to the Admiralty to prepare the Navy for war and Lloyd George wrote to him: 'The thunderclouds are gathering.' At home the rise in the cost of living brought industrial unrest to explosion point. Pits, ports and railways were brought to a standstill by strikes. The East End was aflame with the dockers' strike. The protests of a small band of middle-class and aristocratic ladies, however fanatical, seemed small beer by comparison.

In desperation the Government began to turn against its own promises. In December 1911 Churchill wrote to the Liberal Chief Whip:

We are getting into very great peril over Female Suffrage . . . the Franchise Bill will not get through without a dissolution if it contains a clause adding 8,000,000 women to the electorate . . . The King will disown the Ministry and Parliament will be dissolved on the old Plural Voting Register. What a ridiculous tragedy . . . if this strong government and party were to go down on Petticoat politics! And the last chance of Ireland – our loyal friends – squandered, too! It is damnable.

The Irish Nationalists were now outright opponents of women's suffrage, fearing that it would precipitate a general election and a change of government. The King's Speech at the opening of the new session of 1912 duly contained in its list of measures a Reform Bill to give the vote to all men over the age of twenty-one. No mention of women. The limited Conciliation Bill was effectively dead. It is hardly surprising that the women were in a ferment of suspicion.

Christabel had been keeping their emotions at fever pitch. She exhorted her audiences to the fight with passionate references to Joan of Arc. 'We know that, like hers, our voices are of God.' Emmeline Pankhurst, back from her second tour of America, where she had travelled 10,000 miles and spoken in many different places, prepared herself to lead the fray. 'The argument of the broken pane is the most valuable argument in modern politics,' she told released stone-throwing prisoners at a welcome-back dinner. 'The argument of the stone, that time-honoured political weapon . . . is the argument I am going to use.' At this crucial moment a blundering member of the Cabinet, Charles Hobhouse, played into their hands. Addressing an anti-suffrage meeting in Bristol, he told his audience: 'In the case of the Suffrage demand there has not been the kind of popular sentimental uprising which accounted for Nottingham Castle in 1832, or the Hyde Park railings in 1867,' an allusion to the great franchise riots in which the castle had been burned and the railings torn up. 'There has been no great ebullition of popular feeling,' he concluded smugly. The incitement, though unintentional, was obvious.

The Suffragettes responded with an orgy of window smashing. Sylvia described it with relish:

In Piccadilly, Regent Street, Oxford Street, Bond Street, Coventry Street and their neighbourhood, in Whitehall, Parliament, Trafalgar Square, Cockspur Street and the Strand, as well as in districts so far away as Chelsea, well-dressed women suddenly produced strong hammers from innocent-looking bags and parcels, and fell to smashing shop windows . . . The hammers did terrible execution . . . Damage amounting to thousands of pounds was effected in a few moments.

Meanwhile Emmeline Pankhurst took a taxi to Downing Street and broke some windows at No. 10. She was arrested with 218 other women and sent to prison for two months.

In the Commons the Home Secretary was asked whether his attention had been drawn to Mrs Pankhurst's 'inflammatory speech' to the released stone-throwers. He said yes, but it would not be desirable in the public interest to say more 'at present'. But asked whether he did not think Mr Hobhouse's speech was equally inflammatory, he refused to 'criticize the speech of my colleague'. It sounded – and was – ominous. The Government was planning a new type of reprisal that it hoped would root out the Suffragette nuisance once and for all.

On 5 March 1912 police, armed with a warrant for the arrest of Frederick and Emmeline Pethick-Lawrence and Christabel, raided the WSPU office at Clements Inn. The Pethick-Lawrences were duly arrested, but Christabel was not there. She was in a new flat near Chancery Lane to which she had recently moved. The Pethick-Lawrences, Christabel and Emmeline Pankhurst (who was already in prison) were charged with conspiracy to incite certain persons to commit malicious damage to property. Warned of what had happened by a messenger from Clements Inn, Christabel knew the police would not know where to look for her. She had time to think.

According to her own account, she sat agonizing.

I was alone facing a great problem, a crisis for the movement. Those who had shared the responsibility were prisoners. What best use could I make of the few remaining minutes of freedom to guard against the dangers? At any moment the police would come.

Then, in a 'flash of light', the truth dawned on her. The Government was out to smash the movement by arresting the ringleaders. 'The Government's purpose was to hold the shepherds captive, while they did their utmost to scatter the flock.' Worse still, with the triumvirate in prison, the leadership of the flock might pass into unsafe hands. There could be 'the infiltration of our movement by new elements prompted by our opponents, who would put peace, or party politics, or both, before justice and votes for women.' That must not happen.

The arrival of Annie Kenney's sister, Jennie, gave her a breathing space. She was smuggled into a taxi to a friendly nursing home where Suffragette allies dressed her as a nurse and got her a safe bed for the night. 'I did not sleep all night for thinking,' she wrote. 'Suddenly, in the small hours I saw what I must do! Escape! The Government should not defeat us. They should not break our movement. It must be preserved and the policy kept alive until the vote was won.' As a result of her political and legal training, she knew that a political offender would not be extradited from France. She would go to Paris and 'control the movement from there'. The next day, heavily disguised, she took the boat-train to Folkestone. 'The boat started . . . arrived! My foot touched the soil of France. We were saved. We would win.'

Critics have found her account disingenuous. It needed no 'flash of light', they argue, to tell her that the Government would react savagely once property was damaged on an effective scale. That was why she had clung to 'mild militancy' till her hand was forced. Obsessed as she was with the indispensability of her own leadership, she would then have planned her escape. The move to Chancery Lane was all part of it.

Whatever the truth, she was now, as Sylvia pointed out, 'enjoying herself enormously . . . She was mistress of the militant movement, without a single colleague of equal authority to be converted to her views.' She quickly established a chain of command between herself and Clements

Inn, putting Annie Kenney in charge there to see that her wishes were carried out. It was Annie who became her link, bringing her news and carrying her instructions back to London, together with her prolific copy for *Votes for Women*, in which she continued to spell out the Christabel-given line.

Christabel's escape caused an uproar in Parliament. Despite prodigious efforts, the police could not find her, owing, said the Home Secretary, to the 'fanatical loyalty' of the Suffragettes. Outraged shopkeepers were demanding compensation from WSPU funds for the window breaking and tempers were running high.

In April 1912 Sylvia returned home from a second visit to the United States. She had found that the new militancy had not gone down well there, and her reception had been cool. Typically, she was torn between anxiety and loyalty. 'I clearly foresaw the coming struggle – painful and long,' she wrote. But the battle had been launched and it had to be won.

To save the militants from years of imprisonment, or death by hunger strike and forcible feeding, to prevent the cause from being beaten back by a generation, as had happened to many a cause, a large popular agitation for the vote itself must be maintained at fever heat, and the fate of the prisoners always kept in the public eye.

She decided to give all her time to work for the movement, living on what she had earned from her lectures in America.

Back home she slipped over to Paris to see Christabel and offer her services. It was clear that the meeting was not a happy one. Typically Christabel did not even mention it in her autobiography, while Sylvia dilated at length on her impressions of it in hers. They were not flattering. She found Christabel 'entirely serene, enjoying the exciting crisis of the WSPU and her new life in Paris, the shops and the Bois'. This shocked her tortured spirit. 'Paris was relaxation,' she noted disapprovingly. How could they go sightseeing with so many in prison and their mother facing a conspiracy charge? But she could not get Christabel to share her anxieties. 'As to the movement, she was gay and confident; everything was organized; everything in order.'

Sylvia's offer of help was brushed aside. 'Just speak at some meetings,' said Christabel vaguely. 'I saw that, consciously or unconsciously, she did not welcome my intervention,' wrote Sylvia. 'She was so obviously convinced that her own policy was the only correct one, so intensely jealous for it, that instinctively she thrust aside whoever might differ from her tactics by a hair's breadth.' But Sylvia was a stubborn Pankhurst too. Silently she decided that Christabel's rejection of her merely left her freer to go her own way. She left by the night boat, 'unable to endure another day'.

THREE

The New Militancy

Christabel's flight was to puzzle and alarm more people than Sylvia. What was its cause? Was it just fear of arrest and physical cowardice or was it part of a carefully calculated strategy? In any case, was that strategy justified? The argument was to rage for two years in the WSPU.

Certainly the first effect was to remove Christabel from the consequences of the new wave of intensified militancy that she had authorized. When the conspiracy trial opened at the Old Bailey on 15 May 1912, the Pethick-Lawrences and Emmeline Pankhurst stood alone.

Sylvia described the scene with Dickensian vividness.

The Judge in his silk and scarlet, the old men in their blue robes and their red robes ringed with fur, and the heavy gold chains around their necks, the under Sheriffs, with their white lace ruffles and bouquets of flowers and herbs to ward off gaol fever, were all part of a grim burlesque; a caricature of the Middle Ages flaunting a sour, inhuman visage.

By contrast the two women in the dock, 'each with her special charm, serenely determined to make a platform of it'.

The accused did not deny the charges, as evidence was

rolled out as to how they had organized the Suffragette volunteers and instructed them on the most effective ways to damage property. An earlier militant speech by Christabel was quoted, which did not help:

> They say we are going to get heavy sentences. I say we might as well be hung for a sheep as a lamb. Let them give us seven years if they like. I am ready for it . . . we shall do our bit . . . even if it is burning down a palace.

The jury, though inevitably finding the accused guilty, unanimously urged that their 'undoubtedly pure motives' should be taken into account and that they should be treated with the 'utmost leniency'. Justice Coleridge brushed this aside and sent them to prison in the Second Division for seven months.

A battle of wills ensued between the prisoners and the Government. The convicted three declared that unless they were given political status they would go on hunger strike. Asquith climbed down. They then announced that the same privilege should be given to the rank-and-file Suffragettes they were convicted of inciting, seventy-nine of whom were on hunger strike; otherwise they would join them. Sylvia, 'keyed to a pitch of distraction', threw herself into a campaign of protest, organizing meetings, petitions and Parliamentary Questions. One MP described how she had nearly wept on his shoulder in anxiety for her mother. At first the Government refused to budge. There were extraordinary scenes in the House of Commons when the Home Secretary declared: 'Be they leaders or rank and file, forcible feeding will be adopted if they do not take their food.' Keir Hardie accused him of cruelty. Asquith tried to calm the uproar by saying any prisoner could walk out of prison that afternoon if he or she would give a life undertaking to refrain from all militant action. 'You know they cannot,' shouted George Lansbury, the Labour MP, springing from his seat. Striding up to Asquith he thundered: 'That was a disgraceful thing for you to say, sir . . . You will go down in history as the man who tortured innocent women . . . You ought to be driven from public life.' To the Suffragettes he became a hero and a saint.

Meanwhile in prison forcible feeding had begun. Sylvia reported:

Mrs Pankhurst, ill from fasting and suspense, grasped the earthen toilet ewer and threatened to fling it at the doctors and wardresses, who appeared with the feeding tube. They withdrew and the order for her release was issued next day.

The agitation in Parliament had had its effect. Emmeline Pethick-Lawrence was forcibly fed once and her husband for five days (the Government never forgave him for financing the Suffragettes), but they too were released early and retired to the country to recuperate. By 6 July all the hunger strikers had been released.

The second effect of Christabel's absence was that Sylvia seized her opportunity to strengthen the propaganda side of the WSPU's work. She collected detailed statements from Suffragette prisoners of the conditions they had endured – not only forcible feeding, but solitary confinement, hand-cuffing, frog-marching and beating – and sent them in a report to the Home Secretary. When he dismissed the report in the House as 'a tissue of falsehoods', she sent still more statements to the press and challenged him to sue her for libel, a bait he wisely ignored.

She also set about reactivating the local branches, urging them to organize rallies and meetings in their areas. This effort culminated in a mass rally in Hyde Park on 14 July, a date carefully chosen to celebrate a double event: Emmeline Pankhurst's birthday and the fall of the Bastille. In planning her decorations Sylvia joyfully grasped the chance to show her political colours, placing the red caps of liberty on the top of the poles supporting the banners, which themselves echoed those carried in the great franchise demonstrations of the 1860s. A varied number of suffrage organizations joined in, each with their own colours, which added to the gaiety – bars of black and white for the Writers' franchise guild, orange and green for the Irish, green and gold with the red dragon of Wales, the black and brown for the Tax Resisters, brilliant red and white for Labour – all mingling with the purple, green and white of the Suffragettes. Sylvia wrote delightedly of 'the blaze of colour in the park' and of the swelling music of *The March of the Women*, written by Ethel Smyth for the WSPU, 'strong and martial, bold with the joy of battle and endeavour'.

Not for Sylvia the stale old resolution sent from WSPU headquarters, calling for votes for women 'on the same terms as men'. She drafted her own adult suffrage resolution, demanding political equality all round. At a by-election at Crewe she was to launch another act of defiance, helping the Labour candidate to do better than the Party expected by supplementing the election literature written by Christabel in Paris with leaflets bristling with facts about the hardships suffered by local women both in industry and the home. She organized a Women's Day gathering at which there were throngs of working-class women and their children in their best clothes, enjoying the unusual treat.

103

The local Labour Party was delighted and so was Sylvia. 'The women were helping the Party most prepared to support their cause; they were not supporting reaction against progress,' she wrote contentedly.

But events were moving against Sylvia. At the Second Reading of the Franchise Reform Bill in July, Asquith cast off all pretence of neutrality, dismissing the possibility of women's franchise being included in it as 'an altogether improbable hypothesis'. It was the match that was to set the fire alight. Already restless spirits like Mary Leigh and Emily Wilding Davison had launched some acts of arson off their own bat. Now an extensive campaign of secret – and not so secret – arson was organized. Whether Christabel was directly responsible is not clear. Sylvia claimed that the campaign was 'under the direction of Christabel'. Christabel's own account is not precise. But arson there was on a wide scale, which she did not repudiate. Young women lugged heavy cases of petrol and paraffin through the night, setting fire to untenanted buildings, churches and places of historic interest; on one occasion they tried to burn down Nuneham House, the residence of the anti-suffragist minister, Lewis Harcourt.

One of the most flamboyant escapades was carried out by Mary Leigh and Gladys Evans, who attempted to burn down the Theatre Royal, Dublin, where Asquith was due to speak. They attended a performance at the theatre and, as the audience was leaving, jumped into action. Mary Leigh openly poured petrol on to the curtains of a box and set fire to them. Gladys Evans set the carpet alight and then, with the help of a handbag filled with gunpowder, tried to blow up the cinema box. Not much damage was done, but they were both sentenced to five years' penal servitude. Only after intense suffering through forcible feeding were they released.

'I regarded this new policy with grief and regret,' wrote Sylvia, 'believing it wholly mistaken and unnecessary.' She recognized that every effort was made to avoid loss of human life, but was deeply distressed by the attacks on works of art, 'the spiritual offspring of the race'. But once again her feelings were torn. 'On the other hand,' she argued to herself, 'the heroism of the militants, and the Government's extraordinary treatment of the Cause, which had now become widely popular, largely neutralized any harm that incendiarism would work.' So she uttered no repudiation. But when a message came from Christabel telling her to burn down Nottingham Castle – a symbolic repetition of the action of the franchise agitators of 1832 – she flatly refused to do so as 'morally wrong'. Instead she offered to lead a torchlight procession to the castle and throw her torch at it. That would be symbolic enough for her.

But the most important effect of Christabel's flight was that it cut her off from the Pethick-Lawrences and led to the breaking-up of the Clements Inn triumvirate. The story of the Pankhursts' break with their old partners is a brutal one. The Pethick-Lawrences, who had poured out their wealth and energies into the WSPU for six years and whose home in Surrey had been taken over by the bailiffs to pay the costs of the conspiracy trial, returned from a recuperative visit to Canada to find the doors of the Union closed to them and the WSPU already moving out of Clements Inn. They were not wanted any more.

In *Unshackled* Christabel dismisses the matter airily in a couple of paragraphs. She tells us:

On the return from Canada of Mr and Mrs Pethick-Lawrence there was a consultation in France, where I was now definitely established. The outcome of this and a further meeting was the serious announcement that they and we had parted company owing to a difference of opinion as to the policy to be pursued in future by the Women's Social and Political Union.

In her autobiography Sylvia sniffs suspiciously around the edges of the incident, 'with the unhappy belief that the secret militancy, which I regretted so much, was at the root of it'. She found the breach deplorable and wished that both sides might have surrendered some points. 'Yet outwardly all was dignified reserve on both sides.'

Twenty-six years later, in her book *My Part in a Changing World*, Emmeline Pethick-Lawrence put a different gloss on it. She and her husband, she revealed, had long sensed an underlying difference between them and Emmeline Pankhurst, which had not come into the open, 'mainly because of the close union of mind and purpose between ourselves and Christabel'. Emmeline Pankhurst accepted any truce in militancy reluctantly. 'Excitement, drama and danger were the conditions in which her temperament found full scope.' Christabel, on the other hand, agreed with them that they must advance slowly, taking public opinion with them as they went. Christabel's flight to Paris had given Emmeline Pankhurst the chance to reassert her influence over her daughter.

The result was Christabel's conversion to her mother's plans for widespread destruction of public and private property, carried out secretly by Suffragettes who would try to avoid arrest. Summoned to a conference with them in Boulogne, the Pethick-Lawrences were distressed to hear Christabel endorse this 'civil war' policy. They dismissed the disagreement at first as a 'family quarrel', but Emmeline Pankhurst knew otherwise. The family was no more. It was she who urged the Pethick-Lawrences to take a holiday in Canada and who then wrote urging them to settle there in order to prevent further distraints on their property by the infuriated British Government. When they ignored her advice and returned home, she locked the doors on them.

But the Pethick-Lawrences' biggest crime in Emmeline Pankhurst's eyes was that they urged Christabel to return home and face arrest on the conspiracy charge that still hung over her. Her trial, they believed, would be the sensation of the day and its effect on public opinion irresistible. They would launch a great campaign of public demonstrations on a scale never achieved before. 'It had never occurred to us for one moment that she would not be eager to come back at the first moment.' But Christabel thought otherwise. She was happy to accept her mother's concept of their respective roles: she was to stay safely in command in Paris, while her mother bore the brunt of the battle for both of them back home.

If Christabel was uneasy about her unheroic role, she showed little sign of it. In her autobiography she dismisses criticism defiantly.

'Why does not Christabel come back?' was being asked by one and another. 'There is no need for her to stay away any longer. When is she coming?' But she was not coming back at all. In her hard-headed way she had resolved to stay exactly where she was!

But the Pethick-Lawrences had opened a gulf between them and her that could not be closed. Separation was inevitable.

At first the Pethick-Lawrences would not accept

Emmeline Pankhurst's ultimatum of dismissal and insisted on seeing Christabel. But after an unhappy meeting in London which Christabel, heavily disguised, managed to attend without discovery, they bowed to the inevitable. After all, it was they who had always given her her head. There was a further meeting of the four in Boulogne to agree a joint statement and to settle the terms of severance. As Sylvia put it: 'The Union was an autocracy: none of the four most concerned thought it necessary to consult its membership.'

The first the WSPU members knew of the cleavage was the following announcement:

At the first reunion of the leaders after the enforced holiday Mrs Pankhurst and Miss Christabel Pankhurst outlined a new militant policy, which Mr and Mrs Lawrence found themselves altogether unable to approve.

Mrs Pankhurst and Miss Christabel Pankhurst indicated that they were not prepared to modify their intentions, and recommended that Mr and Mrs Pethick-Lawrence should resume control of the paper *Votes for Women* and should leave the Women's Social and Political Union.

Rather than make schism in the ranks of the Union, Mr and Mrs Pethick-Lawrence consented to this course.

In these circumstances Mr and Mrs Pethick-Lawrence will not be present at the meeting at the Royal Albert Hall on October 17th.

The announcement was signed by all four of them.

The audience at the Albert Hall was shattered by the news and by the sight of Emmeline Pankhurst standing without Emmeline Pethick-Lawrence by her side. She tried to reassure them with the words:

In any army you need unity of purpose; you also need unity of policy . . . When unity of policy is no longer there, a movement is weakened, and so it is better for those who cannot see eye to eye as to policy should part, free to continue their policy in their own way.

There were cheers when she paid tribute to the Pethick-Lawrences' services. It was clear that morale had taken a nasty blow. The collection dropped to £3,600.

It says a great deal for Christabel's hold on the Pethick-Lawrences and her power over people (Annie Kenney, hearing the news, had declared 'If all the world were on one side, and Christabel Pankhurst on the other, I would walk straight over to Christabel Pankhurst!) that, hurt though they were by the breach, they never attacked Christabel personally. Indeed, in his own autobiography, *Fate has been Kind*, published in 1943, Frederick Pethick-Lawrence was unstintingly generous to her. Touching lightly on the anxieties he and his wife had had about Mrs Pankhurst's possessive influence on Christabel, he summed up the reasons for the break with a wrily affectionate tribute to them both: 'Thus ended our personal association with two of the most remarkable women I have ever known.' In some ways, he argued, they were very different. Christabel, with her penetrating brain and acute political analysis, appealed particularly to the young of both sexes. Mrs Pankhurst, with her warm Manx blood and moving voice, which she well knew how to modulate, appealed straight to the emotions of her audience. But they had one outstanding characteristic which they shared with Sylvia, 'their absolute refusal to be deflected by criticism or appeal one hair's breadth from the course they had determined to pursue'. For better or for worse, such people make history. 'They cannot be judged by ordinary standards of conduct; and those who run up against them must not complain of the treatment they receive.'

When the manuscript of Christabel's book was discovered after her death in 1958, it was Frederick who prepared it for publication, giving it the title *Unshackled: The Story of How We Won the Vote*, and wrote an Introduction of scrupulous loyalty to Christabel (and also to Sylvia). His only reference to the split was a few careful words:

It is public knowledge that in 1912 the connection of my wife and myself with Christabel and her mother and the WSPU was unhappily severed owing to a disagreement over policy. Christabel deals with this quite frankly and I see no occasion to comment on what she has written.

Emmeline Pethick-Lawrence could not bring herself to be quite so forgiving. 'There was something quite ruthless about Mrs Pankhurst and Christabel where human relationships were concerned,' she wrote in her book. But even she added: 'Men and women of destiny are like that.' And honesty compelled her to admit that at the Albert Hall meeting on the day of the announcement the Pankhurst magic won back the worried audience.

Never did a human being face an ordeal so crucial as that of Mrs Pankhurst on this night, and once again this intrepid woman rose in the moment of supreme difficulty to her full stature. With a voice thrilling with pathos and alternately with defiance of fate, she intimated that though all were to forsake her, she was prepared to fight on alone. Even my sisters, who knew all that was behind the statement and were intensely indignant with her, felt themselves falling under her sway. As for the audience, it rose to the roof with pent-up feeling and enthusiasm. She held it in the palm of her hand.

It was the Pankhurst magic that enabled Christabel to retain her authority, despite her escape. Her presence in Paris had been made known a few weeks earlier and mutterings were soon heard in the WSPU about her pleasant life there. Where did she get the money from to live in comfortable exile? She was certainly not living in luxury – her flat was modest – but she was not living in discomfort either. A French journalist who interviewed her reported that 'as it was 5 o'clock some women friends came to visit her and she rang the bell for tea'.

Some eyebrows were also raised about her connection with her wealthy, aristocratic friend, the Princesse de Polignac. The Princess's lavish house on the Avenue Henri-Martin was well known in Paris as the centre of a lesbian circle and there has been speculation as to whether Christabel too was a lesbian. David Mitchell in his book on her, *Queen Christabel*, hints at it heavily, but provides no proof. Nor does anyone else. From all that Christabel has revealed about herself, it is unlikely that she had any passionate sexual commitment of any kind. Her autobiography is personally reticent. It contains none of the emotional and sensual outbursts of Sylvia's. She certainly developed an intense antipathy to the male sex, but this seems to have been the by-product of her aggressive Suffragette strategy, rather than of any sexual inclination to her own sex.

Emmeline Pankhurst and Christabel were now in complete control of WSPU policy and of their new paper, the *Suffragette*. Christabel kept in touch with her London

"The Suffragette," July 31, 1914.   Registered at the G.P.O. as a Newspaper.

The Suffragette

Edited by Christabel Pankhurst.   Official Organ of the
Women's Social and Political Union.

No. 94—Vol. III.   FRIDAY, JULY 31, 1914.   Price 1d. Weekly (Post Free)

FORCIBLE FEEDING.

Militant Women Tortured—
Militant Men Received by the King.

Cover of the *Suffragette*, 31 July 1914

headquarters through a series of runners who slipped over to Paris, bringing news and taking back Christabel's instructions and articles for the *Suffragette*. Of these Annie Kenney was her trusted favourite, but, when Annie was in turn arrested, another 'powerful personality', as Christabel described her, stepped in: Grace Roe. There did not seem to be any lack of strong and reliable women on whom the WSPU could call.

Sylvia, freed from Christabel's presence, was increasingly following her own policy, in her 'own way'. She had decided to move to the East End: 'the greatest homogeneous working-class area accessible to the House of Commons by popular demonstrations'. She complained that *Votes for Women* had been turned by Christabel into 'Votes for Ladies' and she wanted to rouse the masses to the cause. 'The creation of a woman's movement in that great abyss of poverty would be a call and a rallying cry to the rise of similar movements in all parts of the country.' The East End had already been the source of great deputations and marches to the House of Commons on unemployment and other social issues, and the WSPU had been active there. But Sylvia's personal presence was to bring the East End into the limelight of suffrage activity.

However subjective her claims may have been about the work she did among the East End women, her opening of a shop-cum-office in the dingy Bow Road must have made an impact. The sight of Sylvia up a ladder, painting 'Votes for Women' on the facia in Roman characters gilded in true gold leaf, astonished, not to say scandalized, the neighbourhood. But it aroused their interest too. 'Women in sweated and unknown trades came to us telling us their hardships; rope-makers, waste rubber cleaners, biscuit packers, women who plucked chickens, often too high for canning, and those who made wooden seeds to put in raspberry jam.' It was all in keeping with her experiences with her father in the dingy back streets of Manchester. So was the abuse she got from urchins and others at some of her first women's meetings. Fish heads and paper soaked in urine were some of the commonest missiles. But women began to join in large numbers.

By January 1913 the Franchise Reform Bill had reached its next stages in the House. On 13 January, five days before the women's amendments were due to be debated, the WSPU suspended militancy so that it could not be blamed if they were defeated. But something even more disastrous was to happen. As the debate opened, the Speaker hurled a bombshell, announcing that if any of the women's amendments were to be carried, the Bill would be so changed in character by bringing women's suffrage into a men-only measure that it would have to be withdrawn and a new one introduced. The Government seemed taken aback. Okay, stormed the women, perhaps you did not actually *plan* the disaster, but the least you can do is to withdraw the Bill and reintroduce it in a form that will make the women's amendments possible. But the Government was only too thankful to have escaped a showdown. All it would promise was to give facilities in the next session to a Private Members' measure, if one were introduced. The women were back where they started. At a WSPU rally that evening, the speakers chanted: 'We told you so! The WSPU has never been wrong!'

Protesting in the House, Keir Hardie said, 'What else is left to the women but militant tactics?' They needed no spurring. Even Sylvia, maddened by frustration, threw herself into the fray. Destructive militancy, she recorded, now broke out on an unparalleled scale.

Street lamps were broken, 'Votes for Women' was painted on the seats at Hampstead Heath, key holes were stopped up with lead pellets ... cushions of railway carriages slashed, flower beds damaged, golf greens all over the country scraped and burnt with acid.

The catalogue of small- and large-scale damage was end-less: telephone wires severed; fuse boxes blown up; boat-houses, sports and refreshment pavilions burnt down in-cluding the grandstand at Ayr racecourse; thirteen pictures hacked in the Manchester Art Gallery; grand homes attacked, including the new house being built for Lloyd George, which was practically destroyed by a bomb; bombs placed near the Bank of England and other strategic points. The Suffragettes were really on the rampage. Many evaded capture. Those arrested faced a price list of punishment: up to nine months for breaking windows or the glass over pictures; eighteen months or two years for arson.

Sylvia, joining in, was arrested with her East End col-league Zeli Emerson for window breaking. By this time hunger striking by Suffragette prisoners was almost auto-matic. Appalled by the prospect of protracted forcible feeding, the two women decided to go on thirst strike as well to hasten their release. Sylvia's graphic account of this self-torture in her autobiography is a classic in the annals of the Suffragettes:

On the third day the two doctors sounded my heart and felt my pulse. The senior told me he had no alternative but to feed me by force. Then they left the cell. I was thrown into a state of great agitation, heart palpitating with fear, noises in my ears, hot and cold shivers down my spine. I paced the cell, crouched against the wall, knelt by the bed, paced again, longing for some means of escape, resolving, impotently, to fight to prevent the outrage, knowing not what to do . . .

Presently I heard footsteps approaching, collecting outside my cell. I was strangled with fear, cold and stunned, yet alert to every sound. The door opened – not the doctors, but a crowd of wardresses filled the doorway . . . There were six of them, all much stronger and bigger than I. They flung me on my back on the bed, and held me down firmly by shoulders and wrists, hips, knees and ankles. Then the doctors came stealing in. Someone seized me by the head and thrust a sheet under my chin. My eyes were shut. I set my teeth and tightened my lips over them with all my strength. A man's hands were trying to force open my mouth; my breath was coming so fast I felt as though I should suffocate. His fingers were striving to pull my lips apart – getting inside. I felt them and a steel instrument pressing round my gums, feeling for gaps in my teeth . . .

I was panting and heaving, my breath quicker and quicker, coming now with a low scream which was getting louder. 'Here is a gap,' one of them said. 'No, here is a better one. This long gap here!' A steel instrument pressed my gums, cutting into the flesh. I braced myself to resist that terrible pain. 'No, that won't do' – that voice again. 'Give me the pointed one!' A stab of sharp, intolerable agony. I wrenched my head free. Again they grasped me. Again the struggle. Again the steel cutting its way in, though I strained my force against it. Then something gradually forced my jaws apart as the screw was turned; the pain was like having the teeth drawn. They were trying to get the tube down my throat, I was struggling madly to stiffen my muscles and close my throat. They got it down, I suppose, though I was unconscious of anything then save a mad revolt of struggling, for they said at last: 'That's all,' and I vomited as the tube came up. They left me on the bed exhausted, gasping for breath and sobbing convulsively.

Morning and evening, day after day, Sylvia endured the same agony. Her gums were always sore and bleeding, with ragged bits of flesh hanging loose. After a later prison episode she described the effects of a thirst strike.

There is always a horrible taste in the mouth, which grows more parched as the days pass, with the tongue dry and hot and thickly coated. The saliva comes thick and yellow; a bitter tasting phlegm rises constantly, so nasty that one retches violently, but is denied the relief of sickness. The urine, growing thicker, darker, more scanty, is passed with difficulty. There is no action of the bowels during imprisonment.

It was the physical map of the Suffragettes' extraordinary heroism.

But the worst part of forcible feeding, wrote Sylvia, was the sense of degradation, fear of what was happening to her companions in other parts of the prison, the sense of isolation and the shattering of the nerves, bringing a wild desire to scream. She found that she could bring up the food that had been forced down her by thrusting her hand down her throat and this daily ritual added to her wretchedness, 'choking and straining, the cords of my streaming eyes feeling as though they would snap'. Sleep was difficult. But gaunt and ill as she was, her eyes like cups of blood, she had not yet done enough to secure release. So she thought up the desperate expedient of undertaking a sleep strike as well. Hour after hour she forced herself to walk up and down the cell until she feared her nervous system would be totally deranged. After twenty-eight hours of this torture she was medically examined and released. She stumbled into a taxi to her Suffragette friends' nursing home and was put into bed.

Ill as she was, she managed to write a long statement for the press on the psychological as well as the physical effects of forcible feeding and helped to stir up public anxiety as to what was taking place. Even Conservative MPs joined in the protest in Parliament. The outcry was intensified when the tube was accidentally passed into the trachea of a young girl, Linda Lenton, during forcible feeding, so that food poured into the lungs and she had a dangerous attack of pleuro-pneumonia. The worried Government, determined not to give way, thought up a new idea. Women whose health was suffering from hunger strikes would be 'licensed out' for short periods until they recovered and then taken back to prison to complete their sentences. In March 1913 the Prisoners' Temporary Discharge for Ill-health Bill was hurried through Parliament. Frederick Pethick-Lawrence, still loyally supporting the suffrage cause in what was now his own paper, *Votes for Women*, dubbed it the Cat-and-Mouse Act.

A few brave men protested vigorously in Parliament. Even Sir Arthur Markham, the anti-suffragist MP, described the Bill as 'mean, cruel, unworthy of the House of Commons and framed with diabolical ingenuity'. Keir Hardie passionately declared:

The endurance and heroism that these women are showing in prison equals, if it does not excel, anything we have witnessed in the field of battle, or elsewhere . . . Do not torture them in prison, and feed them as you would a half worried rat in a cockpit, and let them out, and then take them back once more to prison to undergo all these horrors and tortures.

But the Second Reading was carried by 296 votes to 43, 14 Labour members voting with the Government. Hardie's distress at the failure of the Party to mobilize against the Bill was, Sylvia believed, one of the cumulative distresses that led to his premature death.

A new form of torment now awaited the militants and notably Emmeline Pankhurst and Sylvia. There was another surge of militancy, which lasted until the outbreak of war in 1914, as they set out to defy the new Act. Let out from prison on licence, supposedly to recuperate, they promptly resumed their militant activities. The devices employed to evade rearrest were sometimes heroic, sometimes almost hilarious. On one occasion, when the police were on the watch to rearrest Emmeline Pankhurst as she left her flat, a veiled lady emerged from the building with several other people and the police promptly arrested her. Only when they got her in a cab and she eventually lifted her veil did they find she was not Emmeline Pankhurst after all. Annie Kenney, her licence expired, was determined to speak at a big meeting at the London Pavilion. Someone had the bright idea of delivering her to the hall in a large hamper such as an actress would use. The ruse worked: Annie popped out of the hamper and managed to make her speech before the police arrived. On another occasion a prisoner taking refuge in a Suffragette hide-out, affectionately known as Mouse Castle, escaped in broad daylight when a crowd of women, all dressed alike, suddenly rushed out of the door, the prisoner among them, and fled in every direction, bewildering the waiting police.

But most of this cat-and-mouse game was deadly serious. The Act was applied ruthlessly and the Suffragettes' suffering was intense. The women were released only when their hunger strikes brought them to the point of extreme weakness and the period of 'recuperation' was kept to a minimum. Emmeline Pankhurst was one of the worst victims. It was clear that the Government was going to hold her personally responsible for the acts of damage to property, whether she knew of them in advance or not. When Lloyd George's house was damaged, she was charged with 'counselling and procuring' the deed. Sentence: three years' penal servitude. After nine days without food she was released in an emaciated condition for fifteen days. Attempting to address a WSPU rally, she was rearrested. Another hunger strike followed; another short release – this time for seven days. And so it went on, month after month. She was released nine times after hunger and thirst strikes, only to be rearrested when her brief respite was up.

In June 1913 she was even rearrested on her way to the funeral of Emily Wilding Davison, who had lost her life when she threw herself under the King's horse at the Derby. Emmeline Pankhurst too, she assured her audiences, was ready to give her life for the cause. At one WSPU rally she was so weak she had to be wheeled to the platform in an invalid chair. 'Even if they kill you and me, victory is assured,' was her constant message. Sylvia wrote: 'Her sole doubt was lest she might die at too small a price.'

The women's fury was kept at boiling point by the very different treatment meted out to another group of rebels: the Ulster Unionists. When the abolition of the Lords' veto opened the way to Home Rule for Ireland, Sir Edward Carson, leader of the Ulster Unionists, decided to put another barrier in its way: the threat of armed rebellion if the Home Rule Bill went through. The preaching of sedition, gun-running and the training of volunteers by the Unionists was going on openly, yet no steps were taken against the culprits or against those in Parliament who encouraged them. The *Suffragette* drew a bitter contrast between the arrest of Emmeline Pankhurst for incitement to violence and the failure to prosecute Mr Bonar Law ('Ulster will resist and Ulster will be right to resist') and Captain Craig ('It behoves the Unionists of Ireland to prepare and drill'). While out on licence in July 1913 Emmeline Pankhurst told her London Pavilion audience: 'Sir Edward Carson is a rebel as I am. He told us so in Ireland on Saturday. He is at liberty while I am a felon, and yet I and all other women have justification for rebellion which neither Sir Edward Carson nor any other man in the so-called United Kingdom has.' They had the vote as a means of obtaining redress for their grievances; 'Women have no such means.' The final indignity came when Carson and other leaders were received in audience by the King in an attempt to get a compromise through an Irish Conference, while a WSPU march to Buckingham Palace two months earlier in an attempt to see the King had led to violent handling by the police, many injuries among the women and sixty-six arrests. The contrast was unbearable.

Meanwhile Sylvia was also waging non-stop war against the Cat-and-Mouse Act from her East End base. Like Emmeline Pankhurst, whom she followed in and out of prison in their joint efforts for the cause, she was to go on hunger strike eight times before the outbreak of war ended militancy. Always, on her release from prison, she took refuge in the East End, where the people defended her as best they could against rearrest. Weak with endless hunger and thirst strikes, she was always racked with pain. It was usually, she said, the second day after her release that she suffered 'an absolute collapse; twenty-four hours of blinding headache and acute illness of the whole frame'. She carried on her work from a bed in a humble, vermin-infested home in the East End, writing articles, giving interviews and planning how to elude the detectives to get to her next meeting. On one occasion she reached her destination in a wood cart, tied up in a sack and hidden under a pile of wood. On another she went disguised in poor clothes, carrying a 'baby' stuffed with newspaper. Sometimes she had to be carried to the meeting in a chair and dosed with brandy before she got up to speak. One of her bodyguards was the East End prizefighter 'Kosher' Hunt.

For Christabel, still living in Paris, it was becoming increasingly tricky to justify urging other women to face suffering. True, her Paris flat was a welcome refuge for her mother and other W S P U leaders needing to recuperate after a bout of hunger striking, but those who visited her could not help noticing that she was prettily dressed and growing plump. Loyal as her supporters still were, the contrast with the gaunt faces of the hunger strikers was becoming dangerously obvious. But she remained shrilly defiant of the demands coming from some quarters of the W S P U that she should return home. Once again she vindicated her decision in her book, rejecting the idea that 'the exile' would have been of more use in prison in London than in charge in Paris.

The Exile was flattered as being 'indispensable in London'. She was taunted with cowardice in keeping away. Nothing moved her. As I told one kind visitor who begged me to return with her: 'I could not do it. It is as though a high, hard wall stood between me and that boat. I must not go!'

The nature of that 'high wall' has been the subject of controversy. Was it dislike of martyrdom or the single-minded pursuit of a high strategy?

With Christabel in exile it was becoming increasingly difficult to keep up momentum. Progress through legislation seemed indefinitely blocked. The circulation of the *Suffragette* dropped to 10,000 a week as Christabel's journalistic tirades against the Government's callousness and about women's wrongs became repetitive. The *Suffragette* propaganda needed a new fillip and, as Christabel was not prepared to follow Sylvia's road of linking it to wider political demands, she turned to a more titillating alternative: sex. The woman's vote was needed, she now argued, to purify men. Women had a moral role to fill in cleansing society. 'Votes for Women and Chastity for Men' became her new slogan, plastered across the pages of the *Suffragette*.

It had some honourable antecedents. From its earliest days the women's movement had been concerned with the sexual exploitation of women by men in all its forms – from prostitution to marriage. In the previous century the formidable suffragist pamphleteer Annie Besant had evoked the vision of a 'nobler idea of marriage union', in which men and women would merge their qualities on the basis of mutual respect, so that 'man shall grow tenderer and woman stronger, man more pure and woman more brave and free'. Josephine Butler, wife of a clergyman, had roused the nation with her campaign to repeal the Contagious Diseases Act, which provided for the compulsory medical examination of prostitutes and suspected prostitutes in garrison towns to protect the soldiers – a perfect example of Victorian hypocrisy. But Christabel was to give this time-honoured campaign against the sexual exploitation of women a new and unhealthy twist.

Public alarm was already growing at the increase in prostitution, the reports of a 'white slave traffic' in young girls, the growth of venereal disease and the number of illegitimate births. A Moral Crusade was on the march again. In 1912 a 'white slave traffic' Act had provided stiff measures against brothel-keepers and flogging for procurers. In 1913 a Royal Commission on Venereal Diseases was set up. Christabel seized the opportunity to latch the new mood to her own campaign: to portray man's lusts as the enemy of society, impulses that could be held in check only by giving women the vote.

The Scylla and Charybdis of the Working Woman, postcard, *c.* 1910–14

She began sensibly enough, with leading articles in the *Suffragette* exposing the different standards of morality for men and women, though here again hyperbole began to creep in:

We say to the men who shudder at the thought of a letter lost and a house burnt, make haste to redeem your own sex. Because, be sure of this, women will not tolerate the defilement and destruction of their sisters [by white slavery].

Emmeline Pankhurst used her Old Bailey trial speech to denounce the different punishments allotted to militants and men who abused women.

I was sent to Holloway prison the first time for six weeks for breaking a pane of glass valued at 3/–, classed as an ordinary prisoner, treated as an ordinary prisoner, while a man in the city I know very well, occupying a high position, was sent for six weeks in the First Division for having corrupted several little girls.

When she looked like naming names ('I may not tell you of a judge of Assize who was found dead in a brothel . . .') the judge shut her up. Gradually Emmeline Pankhurst's purity campaign increased in virulence. By July 1913 she was telling her London Pavilion audience: 'The first people to whom you want to apply the White Slave Traffic Act is the Government . . . The Government wants things to be hushed up because there are too many tarred with the same brush.'

Finding that the new morality line was reviving interest in the WSPU, Christabel capped all her previous efforts by launching in 1913 a series of articles in the *Suffragette* designed to prove that 'Man is not "the lord of creation", but the exterminator of the species.' Later in the year Emmeline Pankhurst reprinted the articles as a book, *The Great Scourge and How to End It* – the great scourge being venereal disease, directly due to the sexual vice of men. This sexual vice, she maintained, was rampant in all classes, with 75 per cent to 80 per cent of men being affected with one form of venereal disease before marriage (20 per cent with syphilis), making marriage dangerous. Innocent wives were infected by their husbands, passing terrible handicaps on to their children. All the ills of women, from miscarriage and infant mortality to backache and menstrual troubles, could be traced to men's sexual incontinence. Her details were graphic:

A bride struck down by illness within a few days, or within a few weeks, of her wedding day is told by her husband and the doctor that she is suffering from appendicitis, and under cover of this lie her sex organs are removed without her knowledge.

These horrific facts were 'a warning to men to abstain from vice and a warning to women of the grave danger of marriage so long as the moral standards of men continue to be lower than their own'.

In one article, 'Chastity and the Health of Men', Christabel dilated at great length on men's physiology. She quoted medical authorities to refute the suggestion from some quarters that 'if the organs were not regularly exercised they would become atrophied'. She called in aid the late William Acton, MRCS, to testify: 'I have, after many years' experience, never seen an instance of atrophy of the generative organs from this cause . . . It arises in all instances from the exactly opposite cause – early abuse; the organs become worn out.' W. J. Jacobsen, a surgeon at Guy's Hospital, was quoted as advising that decent men could get rid of an oppression of semen 'by an involuntary emission during sleep once or twice a month, a state of things which is perfectly natural'. Dr J. F. Scott summed it up: 'The proper subjugation of the sexual impulses and the conservation of the complex seminal fluid, with its wonderfully invigorating influence, develop all that is best and noble in men.'

The British public of 1913 were not used to reading such things in a weekly paper – certainly not in a women's paper. Inevitably the articles caused a great stir. Some reviewers lauded Christabel's courage in bringing them into the open so frankly. Others were not so sure. One of the latter was the writer Rebecca West, who, though a convinced supporter of votes for women, was not altogether happy about the tactics of the Suffragettes and teased them gently in wittily mocking articles in the Labour papers the *Daily Herald* and the *Clarion*. This time she was perturbed.

It is long since one objected to the public discussion of venereal diseases, but I believe that Miss Pankhurst discusses them in a way that will defeat her own ends. We are playing the game against ourselves, if we shock the body out of its fastidiousness by coarse description.

Above all she deplored Christabel's 'rancour against men'. The report of the Royal Commission on Venereal Diseases, published in 1916, was to show that, bad though the situation was, Christabel had exaggerated. But the public's flagging interest revived. The circulation of the *Suffragette* soared. Clergymen became ardent supporters of the WSPU.

Sylvia found the new line distasteful. 'Christabel was now, in effect, preaching the sex war deprecated and denied by the old Suffragists,' she wrote in her autobiography. 'In the East End, with its miserable housing, its ill-paid casual employment and harsh privations bravely borne by masses of toilers, life wore another aspect.' To reduce infant and maternal mortality, social improvements like better wages and housing, maternity clinics and welfare centres were needed. But the disagreement between the sisters was not only political: there were deep differences of personality. Emmeline Pethick-Lawrence had christened Christabel 'the Maiden Warrior' and it was becoming clear that a maiden she would remain. For all her prettiness there was a strange sexlessness about her. She attracted men – there were rumours that Frederick Pethick-Lawrence's interest in her had been more than paternal, while radical journalists like

H. W. Nevinson positively drooled over her – but she was not sexually attracted in return. The adoration of a man did not hold any appeal: she thrived on the adoration of audiences.

Ironically, it was Sylvia, the less favoured one, who was the more sensually alive. Plain she may have been, but men responded to her emotional intensity. According to her book, more than one pass was made at her, but she remained single-mindedly loyal to her great love, Keir Hardie. Though she deals with their relationship discreetly in her book, it is clear that their love was physical as well as political. This is confirmed by her letters to him from America, which have been preserved in the Institute of Social History in Amsterdam. Scribbled in pencil on torn-out pages of a note-book as she travelled hundreds of miles by train, they revealed the two sides of her nature. She wrote pages of detail about her meetings, with critical comments on American society, and then the passionate woman came breaking through. From St Louis: 'My darling, I am longing to be in your arms away from it all. There doesn't seem to be anything I can do to alter things.' From Boston: 'How is my darling? I am homesick for the want of you . . . Oh Dear, I don't want anyone but you, but I want you so.' From Mexico: 'It is beautiful, glorious in its immensity yet awful in its lonely space . . . Out there in the sand I could fling myself to the earth and weep out my heart and die in a passion of sorrow and yet Dear if you were there I should see it with different eyes.' On board ship: 'I longed so much to have my arms around you. I wanted to wake you with kisses and tell you I was there.' Keir Hardie's replies to his 'Sweetheart' were more restrained, but they gave her the reassurance that she needed.

The temperamental differences between the sisters were

bound to lead to an open and official break. The only surprise was that it was so long in coming. Sylvia was becoming more deeply involved with the social and industrial unrest with which the country was now inflamed and with the militancy of the new trade unionism. Her final crime in Christabel's eyes was her agreement to speak at an Albert Hall meeting in November 1913, organized by George Lansbury, which called for the release of James Larkin, fiery leader of the Irish Transport and General Workers' Union, arrested for incitement when his Dublin workers were locked out by the employers. 'The Dublin lock-out was to me a poignant incident in our common struggle for a fairer and more humane society,' she explained and went out of her way in her speech at the meeting to quote one of Emmeline Pankhurst's old sayings: 'Behind every poor man there stands a still poorer woman.' Christabel was not impressed. Ironically, one of the Dublin workers' supporters who helped to organize strike soup kitchens was Constance Markievicz, who in 1918 was to become the first woman to be elected to Parliament, though as a Sinn Feiner she refused to take her seat.

In January 1914 Sylvia was summoned to Paris to face a demand by Christabel that the East London Federation must sever its connection with the WSPU. This had long been Christabel's secret aim. She wrote of her arrival in London seven years earlier:

Surveying the London work as I saw it, I considered that in one sense it was too exclusively dependent for its demonstrations upon the women of the East End . . . The House of Commons, and even its Labour members, were more impressed by the demonstrations of the feminine bourgeoisie than of the feminine proletariat.

According to Sylvia's account of their meeting, Christabel

complained of her involvement with Lansbury and with working women. 'We want picked women, the very strongest and most intelligent!' She objected to the democratic constitution of the East London Federation: 'we do not agree with that'. Finally she pointed out that Sylvia had her own ideas: 'We do not want that: we want all our women to take their instructions and walk in step like an army!' There must be a clean break and the Federation must take another name. Sylvia acquiesced silently. 'I was oppressed by a sense of tragedy, grieved by her ruthlessness.'

Oddly, in her own account of this period Christabel made no mention of the break, nor of the meeting which so distressed Sylvia. In fact, her references to her sister were scant and short, while Sylvia agonized at length in her book over their relationship. It was clear that all their lives Christabel was more in Sylvia's thoughts than Sylvia was in Christabel's. It was as though the latter's childhood power over her sister was never broken. Even at the height of their disagreement over the sex-war line, an almost reluctant tribute to Christabel was drawn out of Sylvia. 'Yet, withal, one must say: she was the true begetter of the militant movement, though others bore a greater share of the physical suffering of its travail.'

The casting off of the East London Federation was duly announced in the *Suffragette*. 'The WSPU', wrote Christabel, 'is a fighting organization, it must have only one policy, one programme and one command. The WSPU policy and the programme, and the word of command, is given by Mrs Pankhurst and myself.' Sylvia's Federation became, to Emmeline Pankhurst's annoyance, the East London Federation of the Suffragettes and it launched its own paper, the *Workers' Dreadnought*. Sylvia's East End activities went on unchecked.

In Europe international tension was heightening. Keir Hardie was much abroad, trying to rouse European workers, and particularly the Germans, to resist the threat of war. At home the Suffragettes redoubled their militancy. 'The destruction wrought in the seven months of 1914, before the war, excelled that of the previous year,' claimed Sylvia. Three Scottish castles were destroyed by fire. The Carnegie library in Birmingham was burnt. The Rokeby Venus was slashed in the National Gallery. A bomb exploded in Westminster Abbey. The organ in the Albert Hall was flooded. The destruction of church property was becoming serious.

In May 1914 Sylvia, out on licence under the Cat-and-Mouse Act, decided to organize a great East End women's deputation to the Prime Minister. He refused to receive it. This time she decided that, when she was rearrested, she would go on hunger and thirst strike again and continue it until the Prime Minister received them, or till death if necessary. She wrote to Asquith warning him of her intention. He still refused to budge. Released on 18 June after another spell in prison, she declared herself ready to carry out her threat. Her friends drove her, already weak from the hunger strike, to the House of Commons and laid her down near St Stephen's entrance, where she insisted she would stay until Asquith received them or until she died. As policemen hesitated about what to do, Keir Hardie, who had been intervening for her, came out to say Asquith had relented: he would receive a deputation of six women the following day. Women crowded round Sylvia, laughing and cheering: 'We are winning! At last we are winning!'

Whether this development did, as Sylvia believed, mark the turning of the tide, it is hard to say. Certainly the six East End women on the deputation made the most of their opportunity. They regaled the Prime Minister with facts about the harshness of their lives, and their sweated wages. Mrs Savoy, a brush-maker, plonked in front of him a brush which she had been paid $1\frac{1}{4}$d to make, declaring: 'I do all the work; I keep my home; I ought to have the vote for it!' Unanimously they pressed the demand: the vote for every woman over twenty-one.

The Prime Minister listened carefully. He seemed impressed by what they said about women's working conditions, pointing out that his Government had passed the Trade Boards Act with this in mind. He personally had always been in favour of women factory inspectors. He entirely agreed with them that, if women were to be given the vote, they must be given it on the same terms as men. Though he gave no pledge of action, the women were convinced that his attitude was softening. Nonetheless militancy continued.

Eight weeks later the country was at war.

FOUR

War

Christabel was alone in Paris when the armies began to
march. She left the deserted city to return home, secure in
the knowledge that the Government would have other
things to think of now than hounding her. In any case
there was no need. After a hurried consultation with her
mother, Christabel suspended militancy for the duration of
the war. 'This was national militancy. As Suffragettes we
could not be pacifists at any price. We offered our service
to the country and called upon all our members to do like-
wise.' The women's campaign must wait till the war was
won.

Sylvia was in Dublin, carrying out an investigation into
industrial unrest. She too returned home immediately,
though in a very different mood. The night boat was
crowded with soldiers from Ireland. Men, drunk and sober,
were shouting and fighting. People on the quayside were
cheering and waving. This was the war she had dreaded,
and from which she was to spend the next four years in
critical detachment.

The two sisters were now to go openly different ways.
Christabel's first speech on her return was about the
'German peril'. Emmeline Pankhurst toured the country,

handing out white feathers to young men in civilian dress. Her battle-cry was an attack on enemy aliens: 'Intern them all.' The *Suffragette* reappeared as a pro-war paper called the *Britannia*. The campaign for women's suffrage was put into cold store.

To Sylvia this was a tragic betrayal of the campaign to bring 'the mother-half of the nation' into public life. Hadn't they always argued that women would stand for peace? To her the war was not noble, but a 'huge and shameful loss to humanity'. While her mother and sister made their peace with their old enemy Lloyd George, now Minister of Munitions, and co-operated with him in a campaign to get women into the munitions factories, Sylvia was organizing and speaking at anti-conscription rallies. Hearing of her activities while on a visit to America, Emmeline Pankhurst sent a cable to WSPU headquarters: 'Strongly repudiate Sylvia's foolish and unpatriotic conduct. Regret I cannot prevent use of name. Make this public.'

Conscription of men did one thing for women: it made their war work essential. Sylvia noted in her book *The Home Front* that smart women were now appearing as chauffeurs and skirts were getting shorter. But for her East End women, war brought intense suffering. Prices shot up and so did unemployment, as factories were shut down. Separation allowances for soldiers' wives were meagre. The illegitimate war babies were left unprovided for. Sylvia set up a chain of cost-price restaurants, mother-and-infant welfare centres, a toy factory for unemployed women and girls; she converted a disused public house, The Gunmaker's Arms, into a clinic, day nursery and Montessori school. She took up hardship cases with government departments and led deputations for equal pay. In fact, she was operating as an MP would do.

On a visit to France to look at hospitals she ran into her mother. 'She would speak of nothing but the war,' wrote Sylvia. 'She demanded suddenly "What are you doing?" with a strain of contemptuous irony in her voice.' Sylvia replied that she was working in the East End. 'We were distant from each other as though a thousand leagues had intervened. I was glad to get away, exhausted by sorrow.'

In this new situation the two sisters were working out the destiny dictated by their characters with almost the inevitability of a Greek tragedy. Christabel's love of leadership found happy expression in her rousing support of the war effort: her call to smash Germany into the ground, her relentless pursuit of alleged 'pro-Germanism' in high places. At one point attempts were made by the authorities to suppress the *Britannia* for its persistent attacks on what it called the 'Government of Traitors', but when Lloyd George became the wartime Prime Minister, Christabel backed him with the same headlong enthusiasm as she had once hounded him. Her patriotism won the admiration of Lord Northcliffe, the newspaper magnate. As the war drew towards an end, she turned the WSPU into the Women's Party, with a social programme laced with authoritarian paternalism. In peace as in war there must be Leaders and Led: the concept of workers' control, then being mooted in the wake of the Russian revolution, was anathema to her.

She also managed to have a comfortable war. At her first meeting on her return from Paris, the *Star* reporter noted:

The slight, cool, dainty lady is more beautiful than when she went away. Then the turmoil and the bitterness of the suffrage war were beginning to harden the lines of that small pugnacious face; but the long rest in Paris has restored the beauty that we knew when she first appeared among us.

She was soon launched on a six-month tour of America, not so much to preach women's suffrage as to nag the Americans into joining the war. There too her fresh prettiness was the big talking point. At a great meeting at the Carnegie Hall the *New York Tribune* described her as

a pink-cheeked slip of a girl with fluffy yellow hair and a gown of white satin and pink chiffon. She looked so dainty and appealing that more than one woman in the audience was moved to say that she didn't see how Asquith could have done it.

Christabel also reopened a base in Paris – her favourite haunt – until Annie Kenney insisted that she came back.

By contrast, Sylvia, with her heavy face, short bobbed hair and soulful eyes, was the very epitome of righteous suffering. 'Sorrow' and 'exhaustion' peppered her writing, coupled with moments of exaltation from the intensity of her beliefs. 'Intensity' was her hallmark and it led her into some less happy manifestations: a touch of priggishness, disregard for her appearance, a tendency to over-dramatize and failures of judgement: as when she ruined an interview with Lloyd George at a crucial moment just before the war by arriving 'exhausted', having decided not to take a taxi in order to economize. 'At once I felt that the interview would not be a success; I was too tired to get behind his defences.' Sylvia was her father's daughter, influenced all her life by his admonition to his children: 'Drudge and drill! Drudge and drill!', while Christabel was the fulfilment of all her mother's romanticized hopes and dreams.

Sylvia was interested not in winning the war but merely in establishing the new social order she wanted to follow it. The overthrow of the Czars in Russia in 1917 stirred the Western world. With official blessing, Emmeline Pankhurst travelled to Moscow to urge the Kerensky provisional Government to keep Russia in the war. The Bolshevik uprising a few months later soon put a stop to that. To Sylvia the Bolsheviks offered new hope of a better world and she began campaigning for the creation of a system of working-class Soviets in Britain to replace what she now considered the effete, bourgeois, do-nothing Parliament. She had formed a Women's Peace League and in 1915 attended the International Congress of Women for Peace at The Hague, pressing for a negotiated peace.

She was now to be struck another cruel blow. Attending one of her great rallies in Trafalgar Square on 26 September 1915, she heard the newsboys cry: 'Death of Keir Hardie!' Shocked and trembling, she read it on the posters too. She knew he had been ill, an illness which, she firmly believed, had been precipitated by his agonizings over the war as a pacifist, but the finality of the announcement shattered her. The meeting, of course, went on; the necessary resolutions were drafted and carried. She spent the following day writing an article about him for the *Workers' Dreadnought* and refusing to see anyone, 'my sole respite for mourning and tribute to this great friend'. Then back to work.

But Keir Hardie had been more than a friend. Among her papers in Amsterdam is a poem, scribbled as usual on rough paper. It has no date or title, but the subject is obvious:

> Dear face, so fond to me,
> Rugged with thought, with many lines of pain,
> And with the milk of human kindness filled . . .
> Dear arms that hold me close, dear healing hands,
> Dear breast on which my head rests when I'm tired,
> To which I cling and sob my sorrows out . . .

'Sorrows' again: she never knew how to take life lightly.

As the war pursued its bloody course, what Sylvia called the 'extreme jingoes' began demanding votes for the men at the front. Since the general election had been postponed, the move had merely a propaganda effect, but it started the franchise argument up again. In August 1916 Asquith startled the House of Commons by declaring that, if the franchise were to be extended, women had an 'unanswerable' case for being included. 'During this war the women of this country have rendered as effective service in the prosecution of the war as any other class of the community.' Sylvia, on behalf of her Workers' Suffrage Federation, wrote immediately to congratulate him. Emmeline Pankhurst and Christabel saw it as another trick, complaining that Asquith, having previously attempted 'to use the men to dish the women, was now 'using the women to dish the men'. The fighting men came first and women were prepared to wait. Nonetheless a Speakers' Conference was created to draw up an agreed scheme.

In February 1917 it published its report. It recommended votes for all men over twenty-one and for women over thirty who were university graduates, or local government electors (i.e. owners or tenant householders), or the wives of both. Sylvia attacked this blatant discrimination. To her disgust, the other suffrage groups meekly accepted it. The Government put up little resistance to the ensuing Bill, even when it was extended to the wives of all voters. In January 1918 the Representation of the People Bill became law with overwhelming majorities. Even the Lords showed no fight.

So the rampaging, violent Suffragette campaign died quietly. 'It did not trouble us too much that absolute equality had not been attained,' wrote Frederick Pethick-Lawrence later. For one thing, eight and a half million women were enfranchised, compared with the one million who would have got the vote under Christabel's limited suffrage Bill. And most women, with the new confidence in themselves which the war had brought them, did not mind letting the male ego have its last fling. Ten years later, almost without effort, the last political restrictions on women were swept away.

FIVE

The Final Years

Before the Armistice was signed, Christabel was already planning a new career. In the last weeks before the general election that followed the end of the war, Lloyd George threw the women another titbit: the right to stand for Parliament. To Emmeline Pankhurst it was as natural as breathing that her daughter should become the first woman MP. Was she not the leader of the Women's Party that had done so much to help win the war? At first there was some trouble in getting her a constituency. Lloyd George decided to fight a 'coupon' election in which candidates approved by him and his Conservative colleagues would fight on a co-alition ticket, carrying his letter of sponsorship. Emmeline Pankhurst busied herself getting Lloyd George's 'coupon' for Christabel, and their old enemy obliged, assuring Bonar Law that the Women's Party 'have fought the Bolshevist and Pacifist element with great skill, tenacity and courage'. After intense manœuvrings she also succeeded in getting the Conservative candidate for Smethwick to stand down in Christabel's favour, leaving the field clear for her to fight the Labour candidate.

The election campaign of 1918 was not a happy one. Christabel went down with an attack of the virulent influenza that was sweeping Europe and never regained her verve. The local Conservatives were not too pleased that she had pushed their candidate out. Her opponent, the national organizer of the Ironfounders' Society, was far more at home in the grime of Smethwick than Christabel had now become. The Suffragette rhetoric, at which she excelled, was no longer appropriate and her alternative rhetoric of the 'Union Jack versus Red Flag' variety seemed to misfire strangely. Despite all Emmeline Pankhurst's supporting efforts, Christabel was defeated by 775 votes.

The other fifteen women candidates fared even worse, with the exception of the Countess Markievicz, who won a Dublin seat while in Holloway prison on a charge of suspected conspiracy with Germany during the war. As a Sinn Fein leader, she was not prepared to take the oath of allegiance and so refused to take her seat. It was galling to the Pankhurst pair that such an unpatriotic person should have pipped Christabel to the post – and by a majority of 4,000 too. It was even more galling when, a year later, Lady Astor became the first woman actually to enter the coveted House by winning a by-election when her husband was elevated to the Lords. Nancy Astor was rich, married to an aristocrat and American born. All that might have been forgiven her, but she had committed the crime of never having been a Suffragette or even interested in women's suffrage. Fate seemed very unfair to those who had toiled to get the vote.

Gradually Emmeline Pankhurst's hopes of seeing Christabel in Parliament (and therefore, in her view, automatically in government) began to fade. In the summer of 1919 the Women's Party and the *Britannia* were wound up. Emmeline Pankhurst had no mission left in life and no very obvious means of earning a living. Christabel seemed to have slumped into her old lethargy. When the Sex Disqualification (Removal) Act of 1919 made it possible for her to practise as a barrister, she made no attempt to seize the opportunity. It was as though the propaganda of protest was her sole *métier* and she had no sympathy for the new campaigns for sex equality in all its forms in which Emmeline Pethick-Lawrence, now active in the Women's Freedom League, and others were engaged. She flitted from place to place, writing the occasional article.

Her old friend Lord Northcliffe was of value here. He commissioned a series of articles for his *Weekly Dispatch* under the startling heading: 'The Confessions of Christabel'. Confession No. 1, 'Why I Never Married', reflected her growing obsession with religion. She had not married because she had not wanted to, she wrote. She had stayed single in order to show 'my own personal unending unyieldingness as leader'. She had no reason to be ashamed of her spinsterhood: some of England's noblest women, such as Florence Nightingale and Edith Cavell, had been spinsters, devoting their lives unselfishly to others. Nor did celibacy mean a life without passion. 'I have known passion, passion that strengthens one for endurance, shakes one with its mighty force, makes humans god-like, fills them with creative force.' And all the time she had felt that 'a struggle such as ours had its highest significance elsewhere, was simply the dim reflection of a far struggle on some celestial battlefront where greater hosts than ours clash in the eternal struggle for light.'

During the war she had already begun to show apocalyptic tendencies. The war, she maintained, was 'in very truth a conflict between God and the Devil'. Better to have London destroyed than to make any concessions to

Prussianism, for humanity was not the final expression of the divine will. And she would quote the Bible: 'Fear not those that kill the body but have nothing more that they can do.' This growing religious vein in her speeches and arguments had been influenced by a book she had come across on biblical prophecy. Surely the Second Coming of Christ was a vision cataclysmic enough to transcend and subsume all frustrations and petty mundane anxieties?

It was in this frame of mind that in August 1921, at the age of forty-one, she decided to go to Canada, where her mother had dug herself in as a lecturer. The ability to attract audiences had always been part of Emmeline and Christabel's stock-in-trade and at their time of life it seemed to offer the best prospect of earning a living. But this time their themes were to be very different from the old suffrage campaign days. In the last year of the war Emmeline Pankhurst, with the backing of the British Government, had toured America and Canada, lecturing on the need for women to help the war effort and dilating on the evils of Bolshevism. She had found receptive audiences and, with a Red Scare raging in America, she had decided in 1919, at the age of sixty-three, to return to the lecture trail, flushed with enthusiasm in a new cause. Her travels north into Canada had brought her into contact with a Canadian medical man, Dr Gordon Bates, who had formed the National Council for Combating Venereal Diseases (NCCVD). This was another of her favourite themes and before long she had offered to accept speaking assignments for him. By January 1922 she had joined the NCCVD as chief lecturer and taken Canadian citizenship.

On joining her mother Christabel had no desire to be sucked into her anti-VD campaign. She had other ideas and before long she emerged as a fully-blown Second Adventist, lecturing widely in Canada and the States. American women had just won the right to vote in all elections on equal terms with men after a suffrage campaign of over fifty years, but far from capitalizing on this victory, Christabel was to repudiate it as an illusion and a sham. Still wearing her favourite flowing dresses and big hat, she told her fascinated audiences that the long struggle had been in vain: the sinful world was coming to an end anyway. Some of her former American allies were furious with her, but when, by special invitation, she gave a series of sermons in the Knox Presbyterian Church in Toronto, the audience was so large that the building overflowed. She also published a number of books, showing how expert she had become in Old Testament prophecy and listing the current catastrophes that showed that the Second Coming was near at hand.

Perhaps the most significant of these outpourings from a feminist point of view was her book *Some Modern Problems in the Light of Biblical Prophecy.* In it she abandoned every argument with which she had agitated for the vote. In her disagreements with Sylvia, Christabel had based herself firmly on the claim that only women could liberate women and that women *per se* had a unique, purifying and sanctifying role to play in national life. She therefore rejected Sylvia's party politics. Now she totally recanted her own Women's Party approach. 'Some of us hoped more from women suffrage than is ever going to be accomplished,' she confessed. There was no 'woman's solution' to the problems of the day. Women were not going to pacify the world any more than men had done. 'Human rule is not righteous rule – not even the rule of women voters.' Satanic influences were at work in the world, so there could be no new or ideal order until the return of the Divine King. What could governments do to put things right? Nothing, except believe in the Second Coming.

Intensive lecturing meanwhile left Emmeline Pankhurst exhausted and, after a six months' rest in Bermuda, she turned again to her pet remedy for her financial troubles: opening a shop. Her past unhappy experiences as a businesswoman did not deter her. Overcoming all Christabel's objections, she eventually roped in her old friend Mrs Tuke, who had worked with her for six years as honorary secretary of the WSPU and who had private means. The answer, they decided, would be a teashop on the French Riviera. In 1925 they opened The English Teashop of Good Hope at Juan-les-Pins, taking a reluctant Christabel with them. Predictably, it was a flop. Emmeline Pankhurst's savings were gone. In 1926 she and Christabel returned to London, looking for a livelihood again.

Back on her home ground Christabel continued her revivalist role, but her mother, living very much in the present world, was missing the zest of politics. Her old comrade-in-arms, Flora Drummond, founded the Women's Guild of Empire, which was going from strength to strength. Another ex-Suffragette, Mary Allen, headed the Women's Auxiliary Service, which stood ready to help the Conservative Prime Minister, Stanley Baldwin, to break the General Strike of 1926. Nancy Astor publicly declared that Mrs Pankhurst ought to be in Parliament and that she was ready to give up her own seat for her. All this was balm to Emmeline Pankhurst's patriotic soul, hungry for a cause and no longer obsessively interested in the women's one. She agreed to become a Conservative candidate for the coming general election of 1929.

The Conservatives, delighted at their catch, would certainly have found her a safe seat. Instead, in obedience to some dark impulse, she chose the Labour stronghold of Whitechapel and St George's, Stepney. There can be little doubt that in doing so she was satisfying a desire to challenge everything Sylvia stood for, and on her own ground.

The news drove Sylvia into a frenzy. How could her mother repudiate her father so – and in Sylvia's own beloved East End! She dashed off a letter to the socialist periodical *Forward*, expressing her 'profound grief' that her mother should have deserted the old cause of progress and asserting that she herself had 'enlisted for life' in the socialist movement. She was sure, she added cruelly, that her mother's lapse was due to 'that sad pessimism which sometimes comes with advancing years, and may result from too strenuous effort'.

Certainly the strenuous effort involved in fighting Whitechapel proved too much for Emmeline Pankhurst's enfeebled frame. The East Enders were friendly enough, but her politics were not their politics and inevitably she was frequently heckled about Sylvia's views. Her spirits slumped. The jaundice to which she had been prone since her hunger strikes attacked again and she seemed to have neither the strength nor the will to resist it. In June 1928, one month short of her seventieth birthday, she died, having to the end refused to see Sylvia. In her last speech she thanked Stanley Baldwin for introducing the Bill to extend the vote to women on the same terms as men. To Christabel it was a fitting climax to her mother's life – and to her own account of the Suffragette struggle. In mystical vein the final paragraph in her book ran:

The House of Lords passed the final measure of Votes for Women in the hour her body, which had suffered so much for that cause, was laid in the grave. She, who had come to them in their need, had stayed with the women as long as they might still need her, and then she went away.

She could have added a poignant footnote. The only time she and Sylvia met on family terms during the forty-four years between the end of the war and Christabel's death was by their mother's graveside. An onlooker described how Sylvia, whom her mother had disowned more than once, wept and nearly fainted at the funeral. During all their disagreements Sylvia's extraordinary Pankhurst loyalty held firm. She longed for her mother's affection and approval while not deviating for a moment from the policies she knew alienated her. Sylvia too had the Pankhurst wilfulness.

And like Christabel, she too changed course, though in a diametrically opposite direction. While Christabel was turning from worldly things to the celestial, Sylvia was becoming part of the turmoil of revolutionary ideas that was shaking the post-war world. She adopted the Bolshevik revolution, with a fervour that embarrassed Lenin himself, clandestinely slipping over to Moscow in July 1920 for the Second Congress of the Third International, where she upbraided him for urging European Communists to affiliate to their Labour parties and infiltrate their parliaments. She herself had become totally disillusioned with 'bourgeois' parliaments and the 'bourgeois' parties that participated in them. She was shocked at the idea that she should sully her ideological purity with tactical manœuvrings. Her East London Federation of the Suffragettes became the Workers' Socialist Federation (WSF) and the *Workers' Dreadnought* its

147

instrument. In the same year she jumped the gun on Lenin by rechristening the WSF 'The Communist Party (British Section of the Third International)'.

While her mother had been urging allied intervention in Russia and supporting the blockade of the Bolshevik regime, Sylvia had thrown herself – not without success – into the 'Hands off Russia' campaign. Before long she was in trouble with the Government over seditious articles in the *Workers' Dreadnought*, stirring up discontent over pay and conditions on the lower deck of the Navy and calling for the destruction of Parliament. In November 1920 she was sentenced to six months' imprisonment in the Second Division, having used her trial in good old Suffragette style to hammer home her message that the whole system was rotten and must be changed. Still suffering from the effects of her earlier prison ordeals, she spent her sentence in the prison infirmary. On her release a little band of supporters was awaiting her at the prison gates, carrying banners proclaiming 'Six Months for Telling the Truth' and singing revolutionary songs. She was carried off to a welcoming breakfast – just as in the good old days.

But her independence of spirit was too much for her Communist associates. Lenin paid her the compliment of arguing with her at length in his treatise 'Left-Wing Communism and Infantile Disorder', in which he attacked the ultra-purist, anti-parliamentary line of a small group of 'Left' organizations, of which Sylvia's was the most vocal. Tiny as they were, they wanted to take on the whole system single-handed. Lenin wrote:

It is as though 10,000 soldiers were to hurl themselves into battle against an enemy force of 50,000, when it would be proper to 'halt', 'take evasive action', or even effect a 'compromise' so as to gain time until the arrival of the 100,000 reinforcements that are on their way.

That, he declared, was 'intellectualist childishness, not the serious tactics of a revolutionary class'. With Pankhurst pig-headedness, Sylvia stuck to her views. Her British comrades, exasperated by her continuing tirades against Lenin in the *Workers' Dreadnought*, told her she must toe the line of Party unity. When she refused she was expelled.

Undeterred, Sylvia continued her revolutionary activity by other means. She rejected a chance to stand for Parliament and drew little satisfaction from the fact that eight women were elected to Parliament in the general election of 1923. 'Women,' she wrote, 'could no more reform the decaying Parliamentary institution than men could,' adding, in words that curiously echoed Christabel's, 'The woman professional politician is neither more nor less desirable than the man professional politician; the less the world has of either, the better it is for it.' Her starting point, however, was different: the class war was more important than the sex war. She struggled to keep the *Workers' Dreadnought* alive with the help of funds from friends, but in 1924 was compelled to wind it up.

By now a new partnership had come into her life. In the underworld of agitators in which she moved, she had met Silvio Corio, an Italian left-wing socialist, whose views had driven him into exile at the beginning of the century. Eight years older than Sylvia, he not only offered her ideological companionship, but a veteran's maturity. It was he who ran the *Workers' Dreadnought* when she was away on one of her many trips and gave her the contacts she sought with European socialists. When he and Sylvia moved to

Woodford in 1924, where she bought Red Cottage and opened a café, it was he who ran it while she wrote her endless articles.

In this restful atmosphere Sylvia suddenly decided, at the age of forty-four, that she wanted to have a baby. At the second attempt, and helped by the ministrations of her friends (Charlotte Drake insisted on lending her a wedding ring for visits to the midwife, while the Pethick-Lawrences looked after her and the baby for several weeks following the difficult delivery), she gave birth to a son. She named him Richard Keir Pethick Pankhurst after the men who had meant so much to her. She deliberately chose to have the child out of wedlock as part of her philosophy about marriage: 'I do not advise anyone to rush into either legal or free marriage without love, sympathy, understanding, friendship and frankness. These are essentials and, having these, no legal forms are necessary.' She may also have had pleasure in the thought that by her example she was bringing posthumous respectability to those wretched abandoned women with whom Emmeline Pankhurst had to deal on the Board of Guardians and who had been so persecuted for the crime of having an illegitimate child. Illogically she was deeply hurt when Emmeline Pankhurst, shocked by this final blow, cut her and her baby dead.

The years of rustic calm and motherhood were ones of prodigious intellectual vitality and literary activity. Words poured from her pen: a monumental book on India, another on the future of international language, a review of maternal mortality in Britain, a translation of the poems of the Rumanian poet Mihail Eminescu. Her great classic, *The Suffragette Movement: An Intimate Account of Persons and*

Ideals, was published in 1931, a massive, detailed, vivid and highly subjective account of the years till the winning of the vote in 1918. It was followed a year later by her book *The Home Front*, dealing with the war years. In neither book did she spare her criticisms of her mother or Christabel, though writing about them always in tones of head-shaking regret. The books infuriated Christabel's old Suffragette entourage. Surely this version must not be allowed to go unchallenged? Christabel must write the official one and she must write the biography of her mother before Sylvia beat her to it (which Sylvia did, publishing a sympathetic portrait of her mother in 1935). But Christabel refused to be pressurized. In fact, she had been working secretly on the manuscript that was to be found in a box in a friend's attic after her death. Frederick Pethick-Lawrence, in preparing it for publication, noted that the typescript had been so carefully revised that it was clearly intended for publication, though posthumously. Such reticence was uncharacteristic. It was as though Christabel knew she could not compete with Sylvia's literary masterpiece. And she was right, for her *Unshackled* is a stilted, flat and almost impersonal account compared with Sylvia's descriptive exuberance.

The two sisters were not to meet again after their mother's death. Christabel divided her time between Britain and America, earning good fees for her lectures and from her Adventist books, which were selling well. She was able to live comfortably, helped by a number of bequests from wealthy admirers. Welcome recognition at home was to come in 1936, when she was made a Dame Commander of the British Empire, though even here her satisfaction was dimmed by the knowledge that Millicent Fawcett, leader of the despised non-militants, had been made a Dame ten years earlier. But she was drawing in her horns. When the Second World War broke out, she refused to return home. She had no stomach anymore for patriotic drives, preferring the quiet social round of Hollywood ex-patriate society.

Her last years were spent exclusively in that society. She became a familiar and rather eccentric figure, still wearing her flowing dresses and picture hat. ('I do wish you would throw away that hat,' a woman journalist once said to her.) In February 1958 she was found dead by her housekeeper in her apartment in Santa Monica, sitting bolt upright in her chair. It was the ever-forgiving Frederick, now Lord, Pethick-Lawrence who delivered the memorial eulogy in St Martin's-in-the-Fields.

On her mother's death Sylvia still had over twenty years of vibrant activity left in her. She may have been disillusioned with parliaments, but never with politics. She had a whole new range of battles to wage and causes to embrace. 'Life is nothing without enthusiasms,' her father had said and her enthusiasm for helping the oppressed never flagged. Women were now free, but there were plenty more people in the world who were enslaved.

Under Corio's influence she was to throw herself into anti-Fascist activity. London was full of Italian socialist exiles from Mussolini's Fascist dictatorship and her political sympathy with them was reinforced by the love of Italy inspired by her painting trip to Venice twenty-six years earlier. Her whole being became involved in the struggle for human freedom in all its forms, whether against Fascism in Europe, Stalin's purges in Russia, colonialism in the British Empire, Franco's tyranny in Spain or apartheid in South Africa. The writing of articles and letters to the press, the organizing of protest meetings, deputations and lobbying filled her long waking hours.

She could never refuse a plea for help. Reg Sorenson, her local Labour MP, who died in 1971, left behind him a sheaf of her letters from the 1930s in which she bombarded him with requests to intervene with the Home Office on behalf of endangered Jews she was trying to bring over from Hitler's clutches in Austria and Germany.

Her interest in Italy was to lead her into her last great cause: Ethiopia. It seemed a long way from the suffrage battles of the East End to the court of Haile Selassie in Addis Ababa, but to Sylvia the route was a direct and simple one. Abyssinia, as Ethiopia was then called, was hemmed in by the Italian colonies of Somaliland and Eritrea, and she and her Italian socialist friends were convinced it would not be long before Mussolini, as part of his policy of aggrandizement, would annex Abyssinia. And when he invaded in October 1935, she moved in to rally public opinion in support of the victims of aggression, calling for sanctions against Italy by the League of Nations, helping to found the Abyssinia Association and launching a weekly paper, the *New Times and Ethiopia News*, to keep the issue alive. When, following the fall of Addis Ababa, Haile Selassie arrived in London, she was among the crowd waiting to greet him at the station, and she was to meet him several times afterwards. According to her son, she told him bluntly that she was a Republican and that she was supporting him not because he was an emperor, but because his cause was just.

Nonetheless Haile Selassie's dignity and poise had a father-figure attraction for her. Other allies, like the League of Nations, might throw in the sponge when the Italian

153

conquest of Abyssinia was complete, but she hung on to his cause tenaciously. She used her paper, which the faithful Corio 'put to bed' at the printers every week, to expose Fascist atrocities in the conquered country and to back the guerrilla resistance being organized by Ethiopian patriots. Keeping the paper alive involved a lot of fund-raising work and her last artistic effort was to design the cover of a programme for one of these fund-raising bazaars.

When the Second World War broke out in 1939, Sylvia had no doubt that it was a just war. Her paper, its name changed to the *National Anti-Fascist Weekly*, threw all its resources into the struggle against Hitler under the slogans 'Fascism to be Fought to a Finish' and 'Restore to Independence All Nations Seized by the Aggressors'. The war over, she threw herself into her last major political campaign: the freeing of former Italian colonies in Africa. In particular she fought like a tigress for the reunion of Eritrea 'to the Ethiopian motherland from which it was torn by Italian conquest in the last quarter of the nineteenth century'. She even went personally to Paris to lobby the conference of twenty-one powers that negotiated the peace treaty with Italy. And she wrote a prodigious number of books on Ethiopian problems, all carefully researched and very readable. It was an esoteric subject, but, as always, she made it live in human terms.

The reunion victory won, she became almost the patron saint of Ethiopia, visiting the country several times. Typically, as soon as the political battle was over, she turned her attention to the social and economic one. She had already helped in the arduous task of raising funds to establish and equip the first modern hospital in Addis Ababa, the Princess Tsehai Memorial Hospital, named after the

Emperor's dead daughter. Now she was deeply concerned at the extent of poverty in Ethiopia.

Following Corio's death in 1950, she accepted an invitation to go and live there, but, far from settling down to a quiet life among her beloved eucalyptus trees, she could not rest. She soon founded a monthly journal, the *Ethiopian Observer*, published in Addis Ababa and London, which she largely wrote herself, filling it with material she collected on numerous visits to schools, hospitals and historic sites. Her son described how he and his wife once remonstrated with her as she set off on a particularly strenuous visit to a community school, far from the beaten track: after all, her heart was not strong. She replied indignantly: 'Do you think my active life is over?' Distressed by the number of disabled beggars in the Ethiopian capital, she once again threw herself into the job of fund-raising, this time for an orthopaedic unit and rehabilitation centre.

On 27 September 1960 she died in Addis Ababa. Her magnificent funeral in the cathedral was attended by the Emperor. She was buried in the plot set aside for Ethiopian patriots. Ironically she, who had never been a social climber, ended with the most socially illustrious burial of them all.

She left behind her in England an appropriate memorial to her complex character: her mixture of political professionalism, emotional idealism, eccentricity, self-righteousness and above all, passionate commitment. It was the model of a bomb that she had erected on a plinth in front of Red Cottage in protest at the Italian bombing of Ethiopian villages, which, she maintained, had been made possible by the British delegation's opposition to the outlawing of bombing planes at the 1932 Disarmament Conference. It bore the ironic inscription: 'To those who in 1932 upheld the right to use bombing aeroplanes this monument is raised as a protest against war in the air'. It was unveiled by the Secretary of the Imperial Ethiopian Legation in London. She left it there when they moved. Red Cottage has been pulled down, but the monument is still there.

Two 'musts' for the understanding of the sisters are their own accounts of Suffragette events. Sylvia completed and published her monumental *The Suffragette Movement: An Intimate Account of Persons and Ideals* in 1931. It has been reprinted by the Virago Press (London, 1977, 1984) with a Preface by her son, Dr Richard Pankhurst. The book bristles with facts, personal emotions and shrewd political analysis. When Christabel wrote her own account is not clear. A typed manuscript was discovered after her death in 1958, hidden in an old trunk, and was prepared for publication by Frederick Pethick-Lawrence under the title *Unshackled: The Story of How We Won the Vote* (Hutchinson, 1959). Though shorter and more primly written than Sylvia's, it throws important light on the differences in their strategies and personalities. Sylvia also produced some new details of her earlier experiences in her contribution to *Myself When Young*, a symposium by famous women edited by the Countess of Oxford and Asquith (Frederick Muller, 1938).

Since the Pethick-Lawrences were close friends and intimate partners of the Pankhursts in the Suffragette struggle, it is useful to read their life stories: Emmeline Pethick-

Lawrence's *My Part in a Changing World* (Gollancz, 1938) and Frederick's *Fate has been Kind* (Hutchinson, 1932). One of the more relaxing books to read is *Sylvia Pankhurst: Artist and Crusader* by her son, Richard (Paddington Press, 1979). It gives an insight into the conflict of interest in her life between artist and politician, with attractive reproductions of her artistic work.

The classic commentary on Christabel and her associates is David Mitchell's *Queen Christabel* (Macdonald & Jane's, 1977). It is bitchy and prejudiced but well researched, vivid and stimulating. His earlier book, *The Fighting Pankhursts* (Cape, 1967), gives a fascinating revelation of the Pankhurst family's post-Suffragette activities and reads more objectively than *Queen Christabel*.

Sylvia and Christabel were also prolific writers in their later years. Sylvia's *Home Front* (Hutchinson, 1932) describes her activities in the First World War and was followed by a flood of books on international issues, notably on Ethiopia's struggle for independence. One of the later ones was *Ethiopia and Eritrea* (Lalibela, Addis Ababa, 1953). Christabel produced a number of treatises on the Second Coming, the most illuminating one, showing the complete reversal of her views on the women's struggle, being *Some Modern Problems in the Light of Biblical Prophecy* (Fleming Revell, 1924).

The Pankhursts were very scathing about the non-militant suffragists and it is useful to read the other side of the story. A factual account is to be found in Leslie Parker Hume's *The National Union of Women's Suffrage Societies, 1897–1914* (Garland Publishing Inc., 1982). Roger Fulford captures the atmosphere of the early suffrage movement days in his delightfully written book *Votes for Women* (White Lion Publishers, 1976).

The Fawcett Library, at the City of London Polytechnic, Old Castle Street, London E1 7NT, is a gold mine for cuttings and memorabilia. It holds excellent files of the Suffragette publications *Votes for Women* and the *Suffragette*, and of the Labour *Clarion*, for which Rebecca West wrote some penetrating articles about the militant movement. Christabel's astonishing series of articles in the *Suffragette* on venereal disease, the white slave traffic and other moral issues was published in book form by Sinclair Press in 1913. Entitled *The Great Scourge*, it is now out of print. Fortunately, the Fawcett Library has a copy in its valuable archives.

For those able to get to Amsterdam, the Institute of Social History, Kabeliweg 51, Amsterdam, holds important files of Sylvia's personal papers, which her son assigned to them.